THE ADVENTURES OF SHERLOCK BONES

CASE FILE #2: DOG NOT GONE!

Lauren Baratz-Logsted

Copyright © 2017 by Lauren Baratz-Logsted

THE ADVENTURES OF SHERLOCK BONES, CASE FILE #2: DOG NOT GONE!
by Lauren Baratz-Logsted
All rights reserved. Published in the United States of America by Month9Books, LLC.
No part of this book may be used or reproduced in any manner whatsoever without written permission of the publisher, except in the case of brief quotations embodied in critical articles and reviews.

Cloth ISBN: 978-1-945107-33-7 ePub ISBN: 978-1-945107-34-4
Mobipocket ISBN: 978-1-945107-35-1

Published by Tantrum Books for Month9Books, Raleigh, NC 27609
Cover illustration by Meaghan McIsaac
Cover design by Najla Qamber Designs

For Laura Whitaker:
Terrific editor, friend and human being

THE ADVENTURES OF SHERLOCK BONES

CASE FILE #2: DOG NOT GONE!

CHAPTER ONE

I was having the most awful dream.

Asleep, awake, asleep, awake.

I've taken a lot of flak in my life over how much sleeping I do: the sixteen naps in a typical twenty-four-hour cycle; the naps before and after meals; the naps because it's ten a.m. or three p.m. or even two-sixteen p.m. on alternating Tuesdays –

Well, you get the idea. To this, I say: aren't we all always doing one or the other – waking or sleeping? Unless, of course, we are no longer alive.

And so, since I was most definitely asleep – and that is *perfectly* okay – I was, as previously stated, having the most awful dream.

In this dream, a dog had shown up on my doorstep. Well, actually, he showed up on my lawn, while I was napping outside. He was a Great Dane, sent to me by our mutual friend, and he said his name was Sherlock Bones. He had this wild story about being something called a "consulting detective." Which was a job very similar to being a private detective, or so *he* said. He further claimed that public detectives, the human ones, came to him all the time for help with their more difficult cases, which chiefly involved murder.

Ever since humans discovered twenty or so years ago that animals could speak, they always seem to be asking us for our advice on one thing or another, although they never give us any credit.

Then in the dream, before I knew what was happening, there actually *was* a murder case that needed solving, the human police actually *did* draft the dog to help and I, in turn, was dragged along with them. Then, a whole bunch of other things happened, all so rapidly within the confines of a day that I was barely even able to sneak in one nap, let alone the typical sixteen. Once the murder was solved – actually, we ended up solving two murders before we were done, and did so in a manner so confusing, I barely understood what had occurred – the dog behaved as though he were going to move into my home permanently.

Permanently!

Can you even *imagine* what the neighbors would think of *that*? A dog and a cat, living together?!

Why, it wasn't all that many years ago that the city was still divided into four distinct districts: the Human Quarter, the Dog Quarter, the Cat Quarter, and the Everything Else Quarter. Then, the Great Melting occurred. Now there's even a rabbit living next door. But I say to you again: A dog and a cat, *living together*? Unheard of!

But, in this awful dream, the dog *did* move into the home that had previously housed only a cat – me, Dr. Jane Catson – and my trusty housekeeper/cook, Mr. Javier, a Castilian turtle. Did I mention that, in his spare moments while solving the case, the dog invented a jetpack for the turtle so he could move more quickly from place to place?

It looked preposterous – a jetpack on a turtle! – and I did worry about Mr. Javier's poor little brain as he was always going too fast and crashing into things. Perhaps at some point the dog could create a crash helmet for him? Still, it did have its advantages. Formerly, it could take Mr. Javier days to do a simple grocery run at his old creeping pace. But after the jetpack arrived, he could be there and back again lickety-split.

It really *was* the most awful dream. There was just one problem. When I stretched and opened my eyes as I awoke, I was immediately confronted by the dog from the dream. He was sitting beside me on his haunches, waiting somewhat impatiently for me to arise. As I glanced up at him – this Great Dane, who insisted on wearing his deerstalker hat so often I had to frequently remind him to remove the ridiculous thing – I was forced to admit, yet again:

My "awful" dream … had actually happened. Which meant that I really *had* somehow helped the dog to solve a murder and he *had* somehow wormed his way into my life with the intent to stay.

Well, *rats*.

CHAPTER
TWO

Yes, as much as I hate to admit it, the dog had moved in.

Despite all my protestations, he'd fully ensconced himself in my home – lock, stock and water dish. Incidentally, his water dish alone was so big, it might just as well have been a barrel. And he'd brought all of his dog paraphernalia with him, which included his fencing swords and equipment and his boxing gloves and punching bag. Oh, and his violin and music stand, which he never uses anyway, claiming that once he hears a piece he immediately knows it by heart.

He installed many of these items in my living room, which he always refers to as the drawing room. Before his arrival into my life, my entire home had been an example of cozy good taste. Why, if not for the fact that I valued my privacy above all else, a cover spread in *Feline Architectural Digest* would not have been out of my reach.

Take the living room.

Before the dog, it had a high ceiling – there are high ceilings, which I love, throughout my home – and a stone fireplace with a mantelpiece over it (which you could see from across the room when you turned the corner at the top of the long staircase). Before the dog, the Oriental runner on the staircase leading up from the front door of 221B Baker Street was always pristine. Before the dog, the living room also had two deep-red leather wing chairs that face toward the fireplace from either side, but that could be turned to face the room if company came; a long sofa across the room from the bay window; a floral comfy cushion—also in front of the bay window—on which I preferred to take my indoor naps; an occasional table, upon which lay the black telephone only used occasionally; various personal and decorative items, like framed pictures and such; and a large Turkish carpet covering most of the hardwood floor.

After the dog, the living room still had all those things, but it also had those items I mentioned the dog had brought with him, and – wait for it! – a basket filled with chew toys. Now it's true, although I haven't mentioned it yet, that I keep my own basket in the living room. But mine is filled with classy items: balls of yarn in lovely colors, like orchid, pale pink and lime green; cloth mice, some with feathers attached for variety; and jingly balls, which are balls with bells inside. I love a good jingly ball.

True, they are not the classiest in appearance, but I stow them discreetly at the bottom of the basket, under the finer things, whenever I'm expecting company, which, thankfully, is almost never. But the dog's basket? Filled to the brim with ugly, plastic *chew toys*? Ghastly. The chew toys even *squeak*.

The dog's move in took place over the course of

one very long day. I was so distressed, I couldn't nap. I was so distressed, I could barely watch, keeping my paws over my eyes, only peeking out briefly each time he thumped up the stairs with yet another item to be added to my previously tidy home. He'd even installed two chandeliers, one for the living room and one for the dining area, which you reach from the living room by passing through French doors that are almost always left open. The chandeliers did add a lovely light and warmth, plus a touch of additional class to the place. But I wasn't about to tell *him* that.

Besides, I didn't need to. Because the turtle complimented the dog nearly every day.

"Oh, Boss!" Mt. Javier enthused each day as he set about his duties. "Aren't these chandeliers beautiful?"

"Well, I suppose they're all right," I allowed.

"And wasn't it *brilliant* of Boss," and here I knew Mr. Javier was referring to the dog, who he now thought of – annoyingly – as his other boss, "wasn't it brilliant of him to design for me this jetpack?

You know, Boss, without the jetpack, it would take forever for me to dust the chandeliers."

Each day, as I lazily watched Mr. Javier dust, suspended high in the air by his jetpack as he flitted around the chandeliers waving his little dust rag at the crystal pieces, I was forced to admit he had a point.

If we'd had chandeliers but no jetpack, Mr. Javier would have been forced to drag out the tall stepladder, making his laborious way up the rungs. Such a process could take him all day. But now? In minutes, he could be done.

So yes, I supposed the dog could be beneficial for some things. If only he weren't so annoying about so many other things.

Take, for instance …

CHAPTER THREE

No sooner had the dog installed all his things in my home – *my* home, may I emphasize, since it was my name on the deed of ownership – than he commenced to introduce us proudly to everyone we came across as "Bones and Catson, Consulting Detectives."

No, really. When I say everyone, this is not an exaggeration. We're talking here about people in shops, random strangers on the streets, and any delivery person who came to the back door with, you know, a delivery.

And each time he did it, my mind silently

screamed: *When did I ever agree to* this?

Sometimes, my screaming was not so silent. In fact, it was occasionally quite loud as I sought, repeatedly, to point out to the dog that I had never signed up for any of this … not ever.

But do you know what happened each time I yelled?

Instead of getting angry back – instead of shouting at me in return – the dog would simply sit there on his haunches, gazing at me calmly, until I was quite finished. Then the dog would ask calmly – and how annoying is *this* – "Are you quite finished?"

When one is really angry about something, there is nothing quite as infuriating as the irritating party behaving as though there's nothing worth getting bothered about.

And so, after a time, I eventually stopped screaming and shouting … at least out loud. I simply gave in to it all. "Bones and Catson, Consulting Detectives" included.

But I did tell the dog that if we were going to do this thing, we should do it right.

"I'm sorry," the dog said, "but I don't follow."

"If we're to be in this business together," I said, "then obviously we should put a sign above the door to our 221B address."

"A sign? What sort of sign? Do you mean like one of those hex signs to keep witches away like those that can be found on barns in Pennsylvania Dutch Country in the United States of America?"

"No, I don't mean a *hex* sign! We're not *witches*!"

"Then what sort of sign do you mean?"

"A *business* sign!" I didn't add "You stupid twit" to the end of the sentence but I swear it hung in the air.

"And what would this business sign say?"

"Oh, I don't know." I shuffled my paws a bit, looked at the ground. "*Dr. Jane Catson & Sherlock Bones, Consulting Detectives*, perhaps?"

The dog laughed. "Leaving out the fact that the order of names in such a sign would be inaccurate, both alphabetically and in terms of detecting abilities, we don't need any *sign*."

He didn't say "You stupid twit" either but I

13

definitely heard it in his words, along with a particular scoff in how he said "sign."

It was so annoying. *He* was the one that kept insisting to everyone that we were some sort of partners. *He* was the one who dragged me into all this. And now, the first time I made a suggestion to improve our business – a smart one, I might add – he was shooting me down? You'd think he'd at least be appreciative, *happy*, that I was making an effort.

"Well then, business cards, at least," I tried again. "We should have proper business cards printed up, regardless of the order of our names on the cards."

He stared at me – dumbly, I might add.

"You know," I explained, "our names plus the address and phone number, so clients can locate and get a hold of us."

"Whatever for?" The dog laughed again. "I don't need to advertise or become some sort of ambulance-chaser. Everyone knows who *I* am. The cases come to me!"

I had to admit, the last case we worked on together, it really had just come to him, with a knock at the door and a human saying, basically – *boom!* – "Here's a case." But did he really think it could and would just happen like that, over and over again?

Wow. Someone had an awfully high opinion of himself.

Sure, it could work that way.

The delusional dog could just keep telling himself that.

In the meantime, I'd find some way to do a thing or two my way.

"Fine," I told him. "You just keep telling yourself that."

Which brings me full circle back to where we began. I had just awoken on my comfy cushion beside the bay window in my living room from what I thought was an awful dream of the dog moving in, only to find it real and the dog staring down at me. The glass in the bay window had to be replaced after our last case because the murderer had tried to escape through it. In my worst nightmares, I sometimes still saw my lovely cushion, littered with dangerous shards of glass.

"You know, Catson," Bones said with neither greeting nor introduction, as was his habit, "I've been thinking."

"Well, that can't be good," I said with a yawn.

"I've been thinking," he said, "you need to get out more."

"What are you talking about, Bones? I'm outside all the time. Well, except for when I'm inside, like now. But other than when I'm inside? I'm always outside."

"I'm not talking about the variety of places you nap. Napping on the lawn, I must point out, is not socializing. You should socialize more. You never have anyone in, and so you must get out more."

"I'm a *cat*," I pointed out, stating the obvious. "I like my privacy, which I had plenty of until you came along. I don't need to *socialize*. You do enough of that for both of us."

This was true. Since he'd moved in, he was forever entertaining all sorts of visitors. The Baker Street Regulars, comprised of six Cocker Spaniel stray puppies, were among the most frequent – especially their pack leader, Waggins. What they could do with that basket of chew toys, you don't even want to know.

Also, heaven help me, now *I* was referring to us as an *us*.

Before he could respond, his eyes seized on something outside our window.

Suddenly, he screamed, "Squirrel!"

And then he was racing for the door.

CHAPTER FIVE

Immediately, I raced after him.

Because, well, who doesn't enjoy a good squirrel chase?

The only problem was, I couldn't run nearly as quickly as the dog because, well, he *is* a dog; plus, I have this nasty limp, a holdover from my service in the Cat Wars.

So while the dog bounded down the long flight of stairs, descending from the living area of my home to the door leading out to the street, I quickly limped behind. When I got to the bottom, I saw the dog had left the door hanging ajar behind him, meaning

I could just follow through that rather than having to leap through the rectangular door flap which is my usual method of exit and entry. Some humans call such a thing a pet door, but I am *no one's* pet.

Once outside and down the path, I looked left and right to see which way the dog had gone. He had run left, of course. The dog was almost always going left, just like he'd taken the left bedroom in my home, although now was not the time to dwell on dwelling arrangements.

The dog was all the way at the end of the street, one paw acting as a visor over his eyes as he scanned the horizon.

At last, with a rare and brief look of dejected failure, he trotted back to me.

"Did you see where he went, Catson?" he said, back to his usual urgency.

"Who?" I asked. "The squirrel?"

"Of course, the squirrel!" he said with some exasperation.

"I'm afraid not," I admitted. "By the time I got outside, he was nowhere in sight. But look, there's another squirrel over there. And there. And there. There are plenty of squirrels everywhere this time of year."

It was late summer and the squirrels were all busily gathering food to store for winter. One could almost pity the squirrels their need to do that. Me, whenever I need to stock up, I just send Mr. Javier to the corner store for more tins of tuna and packages of pasta.

I would have started chasing some of the squirrels but, frankly, I was a bit tired after my run down the stairs. Speaking of which, was it time for another nap yet?

"I don't want just some *random* squirrel!" he said, more exasperated yet.

"You don't?" Now I was puzzled.

"What do you think we've been doing here, Catson?" he said with his I'm About To Teach You A Lesson voice. You can imagine how much I enjoyed that voice.

"Well," I said speaking slowly so as to irritate him. If he was going to talk to me like I was an idiot, I might as well act like one. "You got a crazed look in your eyes, yelled 'Squirrel!' and then went racing out of the house."

"And what did that further lead you to deduce?"

"Naturally, I first thought you were a lunatic. But I realized almost immediately that you said *squirrel*. I get distracted by squirrels too. This thought, in turn, led to: 'Now this makes sense' and 'I love chasing squirrels too – finally, something we share in common! Their beady eyes; there's just something about them, makes me want to chase them all the time.' And there you have it."

"Not quite. While I can be as easily distracted as the next chap by a squirrel flashing by, I – unlike you – do not chase willy-nilly after random squirrels."

"Willy-nilly? There's no need to be insulting about – "

"That, my dear Catson, was no random squirrel."

"Oh no?" I said mildly. "Then who was it?"

"It was the villain."

"As far as I'm concerned, all squirrels are villains. But, somehow, I'm guessing we don't mean the same thing."

"I did not say the squirrel was *a* villain. I said the squirrel was *the* villain."

"Seems a bit specific, not to mention a heavy charge," I said, unable to hide the skepticism in my voice. "So, you know that squirrel personally, do you?"

Really, how can anyone tell one squirrel from another? They all look alike.

"Oh, yes," he said with vehemence. "I have known that squirrel for some years now, have been deviled by him regularly in fact."

"Really?" I said, thinking he must be joking. "And who is he?"

"Why, the squirrel is a criminal mastermind, of course."

"Oh, of course," I scoffed.

"He goes by the name of Professor Moriarty."

CHAPTER SIX

I couldn't help it. I burst into laughter.

"What's so funny?" the dog demanded.

"It's just that you – " I could barely contain my mirth. OK, I couldn't contain it. "You … you … you said the squirrel is a criminal mastermind – the *squirrel!* – and that he has … has … has a name and – "

"I fail to see the humor."

"I've never known a squirrel with a name before!"

"That's because you're prejudiced, Catson. If you weren't, you would know that all living creatures have names, if only you pay attention and listen. It's not just cats and dogs and humans and Castilian turtles that have names. Speaking of which … "

The dog was off again, one paw in the air. He trotted over to a horse idling in the traces of a cab on the street in front of our home, traces being the leather reins and such keeping the horse tethered to the cab, shouting "Fred!" like another might shout "Eureka!"

Huh. I hadn't even noticed the horse and cab there when I'd first raced outside, and from the looks of the horse, he'd been there for some time. I could tell that because he wore the bored-with-it-all look horses tend to get when waiting in traces for too long.

I caught up with the dog before he had the chance to engage with the horse, this so-called "Fred."

"How many times have I told you?" I said. "There's no point in talking to horses." In the short time we'd lived together, I'd told him at least twice. "All you ever get out of a horse is 'Blah, blah, blah' and 'Oats, oats, oats' and possibly 'Dude, where's my carrot?' They're useless!"

The horse turned to me, giving me an offended

look from between his blinders. "You don't need to be so insulting about it," he said. "Some of us have to work for a living."

I sat back on my haunches, placed my front paws on my hips. "I resent that! I'll have you know, I'm a board-certified surgeon. I'd still be working at the Cat Hospital had I not been injured in the Cat Wars."

"Ooh, lah-di-dah. He says he's a surgeon." The horse didn't bother to stifle his yawn. "Well, aren't I impressed."

"Not *he*, you stupid beast. *She*. Can't you see I'm a *girl*?"

"Frankly, no." Another yawn from the horse, who turned to the dog with much more alertness than he'd shown me. "What can I do for you today, Mr. Bones? Can I be of some service?"

Mr. Bones? Mr. *Bones*? That seemed like an unnaturally high level of respect to show the dog.

"Yes, please, Fred," *Bones* said, his voice filled with an equal level of respect. "I know how alert you always are and I wondered if you could tell me:

Have you seen which way Moriarty went?"

"You mean the nefarious Professor Moriarty?" the horse said. As he spoke the name, the horse's giant black nose quivered and his ears shot back so they were almost flat against his head.

Wait. The *horse* knew this Moriarty squirrel?

"The very same," the dog said with an earnest nod.

"Oh, I wish I could help you out, Mr. Bones," the horse said ruefully. Huh. I didn't know horses could be rueful. "I do know what a thorn that villain has been in your side all these years. He's been such an enemy to the city, the country – the whole world, even! – but most especially to you, sir."

"That he has, Fred."

All of this "Fred" this and "Mr. Bones" that – it was enough to make one sick. Not to mention …

"Time out!" I cried, raising one front paw straight up and than laying the other front paw flat on top of it to make a T.

"Yes, my dear Catson?" That, of course, would be Bones. I most definitely was not the horse's *dear*.

"How is it possible," I said, "that there is a squirrel at large who goes by the improbable name of Professor Moriarty; a squirrel that not just you, Bones, have knowledge of; and yet I have never heard of him before this very day?"

"I don't know, Catson," the dog said. "Perhaps, as I've been trying to tell you, you need to get out more? Or perhaps, as I've suggested often enough, you might try reading a newspaper from time to time?"

"Pah." I waved a dismissive paw at this last. "I would if they ever printed anything worth reading."

"I rest my case," Bones said, although I failed to see his point. He turned back to the horse. "So," he said sadly, "nothing?"

"'Fraid not," the horse said. "I'd tell you which way Professor Moriarty went if I could, sir. But I never saw him, did I? I was too busy wondering where my next oats might be coming from."

HA! Like I said, there's no point in talking to horses.

"That's all right," the dog soothed the horse with

more gentleness than I'd have suspected the dog capable of; certainly more than I'd have offered the beast. "You do your best."

"I do that, sir."

"And it's possible," the dog said, "that the squirrel isn't at all involved in the case at hand. It's possible that Moriarty is just a mere distraction today. Of course, if not this case, he'll figure into another before long."

I was about to laugh at them again, the very idea of the dog and the horse seriously discussing this Moriarty as though he might really be some criminal mastermind, when everything I know about squirrels hit me:

Devious. Highly intelligent. Incredibly organized. Deceptively adorable to humans. And you never quite know what nefarious things they might be hiding under their bushy tails.

Was it possible … ?

But also:

"Wait!" I made my time-out sign again. "What just happened here?"

The dog and horse turned and stared at me.

"How do you mean?" the dog asked.

"You said 'the case at hand,' not long after followed by 'this case'. Since when was there a case?"

The dog laughed at this. "My dear Catson," he said with a roar, "there is *always* a case!"

Worse, the horse was roaring with laughter too.

"Bones," I said testily, "what specific case?"

The dog turned to the horse. "Have you heard anything lately, Fred?"

The horse cast his eyes heavenward, considering. Finally:

"Well, I did hear someone say *Utah* … "

CHAPTER SEVEN

"*Utah?*" I said. "*Utah?* You mean that dry state that resides somewhere within the western confines of the United States … *of America?*"

The dog and horse exchanged a glance.

"Do you know of another one, Fred?" the dog asked.

The horse shrugged. "Not I, Mr. Bones. But then, I don't have your vast knowledge of geography. Or anything else for that matter."

This mutual admiration society of theirs really was nauseating.

"You can't just pick a place at random," I said.

"It's not like you can spin a globe, stick a pin in it blindly, say, 'Ooh, look, Utah!' and then declare 'There must be a case there!'"

"How is it random?" the dog said. "Did you not hear Fred say he heard someone say *Utah*?"

"Yes, but that's not the point!"

"Which is?"

"The *point* – "

And then, just like that, I stopped myself cold.

My mind harkened back to our first case file, *Doggone*, which I'd written up upon its completion (and which you can also read).

I have a confession to make:

That incredibly long day, during which Bones had solved not one but two murder cases, had all been a bit of a muddle to me. With his weird assortment of expertise, Bones knew things that no normal being could possibly know – and oh, how I hate to admit that. But it was also true that I hadn't paid enough attention to the dog, putting down much of what he had said to leaps of illogic. And yet, afterward, I couldn't escape the feeling that had I only paid closer attention, I could have figured things out too, or even at least understood what happened.

I internally vowed that this time it would be different. If we did indeed have a case, this time I would pay close attention and try to figure this thing out too, whatever *this thing* was.

Even as I made this vow to myself, I could almost hear Bones's voice chortling inside my brain: "But I'm brilliant, so how could you possibly ever keep up?"

I chose, in my wisdom, to ignore that imagined chortling voice and level my steady gaze at my two companions and ask:

"So. Utah. What are we going to do about Utah?"

CHAPTER EIGHT

"No, really," I said to Bones, "what are we going to do about Utah?"

We were back inside in our (ugh, there's that *we* again) cozy living room to be precise. Thankfully, Bones had not invited the horse indoors with us. If he had, our living room would have been considerably less cozy.

"We shall get to that, my dear Catson," said the dog. "But first, I'm famished, aren't you?"

"A bit," I agreed.

"I'm afraid that's not possible."

"Pardon?"

"The state of being famished is an extreme state to be in, so I don't think you can be a bit famished any more than one can be a bit dead. The states of being dead or famished are both either/or propositions. In other words, either you are or you are not, and there is no 'a bit' about it."

"Thank you so much for the language lesson, Bones," I said sarcastically. "Now that that's out of the way, what would you like Mr. Javier to prepare us for lunch?"

He considered. "I could go for a nice Dover sole."

"I'm afraid that's not possible. Mr. Javier has gone off fishing."

"You mean to say the turtle is not here?"

"No, that is not what I mean to say at all. By 'off fishing' I do not mean it in the usual way to imply one is on vacation somewhere. I mean he's gone off the thing itself. He refuses to do it anymore."

"And why is that?"

"He says some of the creatures who live in the water are friends of his and he refuses to be party to their being turned into dinner anymore."

"The turtle says all that, does he?"

"He does, as of this morning. Although, to his credit, he says all of that quite cheerfully, given the subject."

Since Bones had created the jetpack, a change had come over Mr. Javier. Many changes, in fact.

Oh, to be sure, in the beginning, when Mr. Javier first got the contraption, he had trouble controlling the thing. He was forever banging into walls and bashing his head against the ceiling.

But as the days passed and he gained mastery of the device, a new confidence was instilled in him and I noted an increased joy in his work. This made me wonder, guiltily: Before Bones came, had I been a bad mistress to Mr. Javier? But there hadn't been much time for me to feel guilty because with his new confidence in his work, Mr. Javier had also acquired a stronger sense of self-worth. Which had led him to make what were becoming increasingly more annoying demands.

Like the off-fishing thing.

"So, no more fish?" the dog said.

I shook my head ruefully. "Not even a shrimp."

The dog considered. "I suppose there will be a lot of chicken in our future, won't there?"

"Well, unless the turtle goes off chicken too."

CHAPTER
NINE

Thankfully, the turtle had not gone off chicken.

About an hour later, Bones and I found ourselves seated on high-backed chairs in the dining room at either ends of the long table, enjoying our midday meal beneath the chandelier (which did add a lovely glow to the table).

"You know," the dog said, sucking on a chicken bone as he considered our surroundings, "I'm thinking of painting the walls red. I read somewhere that red walls aid digestion."

"You most assuredly will not," I said.

"But I could."

"But I will not let you."

"And why is that? I'm a rather accomplished painter, if I do say so myself. My work, I am told, has a da Vinci flair to it."

"Be that as it may – although I'm guessing that no one actually compared your painting to da Vinci's, whomever she may be – I let you bring your chandeliers and all your other things in here, but I will not let you paint my walls. Changing my walls would be a bridge too far."

"I'll accept that," the dog said, "for now." He picked up and sucked on another chicken bone. "By the way, I do like a fricassee as well as the next chap, but I do wonder if Mr. Javier might not be persuaded to try doing something else with a chicken."

"I wouldn't ask him that if I were you."

"No?" Bones raised an inquisitive eyebrow.

"If you do, he might tell you that we can just do our own cooking from now on if we don't like his."

Bones considered and then came the rueful: "He might say that, mightn't he?"

"The New Mr. Javier?"

Bones nodded.

"I'd say it's a pretty safe bet. Then we'd be left with a housekeeper/cook minus the cook."

Bones threw down the last bone. "Stop dawdling, Catson."

"*Me*? What are you talking about?"

"Don't you want me to tell you about Utah?"

CHAPTER TEN

"I'm not going to tell you about Utah just yet," the dog said, in that infuriating way he had.

"Well, thank you so very much for leading me right up to the thing and then leaving me hanging. Must every conversation with you be a series of cliffhangers?"

"Ah, but I don't find the cliffs to hang things on; the cliffs find me."

The cliffs find me? What arrogance! I was about to point out as much when he made things so much worse by adding:

"I am the world's greatest consulting detective, am I not?"

I rolled my eyes.

"I do understand your feeling of professional jealousy, Catson, but only one of us can be the best. The best is another one of those things like famished or dead – you either are or you are not. And, in my case, I am the best and there's nothing more to say about it."

Now, not only was I rolling my eyes, but I wanted to kick him too, which I would never do. I'm not the violent sort. In the Cat Wars, I didn't fight; rather I stitched and sewed up and tried to repair and save those who did fight. But roll my eyes and want to kick him I did, because not only was what he said annoying to me, but I also knew that last part was wrong. *Nothing more to say about it?* I knew him. If he stayed living here long enough, he'd find plenty more to say about it. Over and over again.

"You were saying?" I prompted. "About not being ready to discuss Utah yet?"

"Why, yes. I thought that, first, it might be best to review the details of the last case we worked together, since that case is tied in to this case."

"I still don't know what 'this case' *is*!"

"All in good time, all in good time."

How infuriating. It was the verbal equivalent of being patted on the head by a human.

"You will recall," the dog said, "that our last case formally began with the murder of a man with a German name."

"Yes, I do recall. And I also recall that at the time, I suggested – and you and the public human detectives all agreed – that we could just refer to him as, er, John Smith."

I have the devil of a time trying to get names of foreign origin straight – really, any human names can throw me – and so I had settled on this as a solution that would work nicely for everybody, especially me.

I also remembered the two public human detectives involved in the case. One was an Inspector Strange, who Bones had apparently had several previous dealings with. Bones and Inspector Strange did not appear to like each other much. In my opinion, Inspector Strange resented that he had a need for Bones's superior intellect and Bones resented that Inspector Strange never credited him for the cases he solved. The other public human detective, a rather quiet chap, I knew only as Inspector No One Very Important, due to the fact that I missed his name the first times it was spoken and it would have been embarrassing to ask for it after so much time had passed.

"Just so," the dog agreed. "And you will further recall that a second murder took place."

"Yes," I said. "We all agreed we could call that second victim the Secretary which only made sense since he was, in fact, Mr. Smith's secretary."

"That is also correct, although the Secretary – an American, I might add – did have a name, and that name is Stangerson."

"Potato, potahto," I said. "Plus, if we start calling him that now, Stangerson being so close in name to Inspector Strange, I shall become thoroughly confused. If he figures further into the tale, can we not continue calling him the Secretary?"

After much thought, the dog nodded. "I will agree this time, to what you think are simplified names, but I do hope, if we are to continue in business together, that soon you will embrace what is accurate rather than what is easiest for your brain."

It sounded to me as though there were more than one insult buried in there. A couple of other things rankled about it as well.

One, 'if we are to continue in business together'? What, was I on trial here? I thought *he* was! Just because I'd let him move his things in, no one ever said I'd let him make this situation permanent. It was still my house.

Two, this idea of a longer acquaintance with him changing me in some way. What about me needed to change? I would confess that since meeting the dog, my limp had decreased both in severity and the amount it troubled me. Perhaps I limped less because he kept me so active. Or – and oh, how I hate to entertain this thought – maybe he was good for me in that he kept me so busy, both in mind and body, I no longer had time to dwell on what was really a minor physical impediment?

But then, hadn't he changed too? When I first

met him, even though so much about him had struck me as strange (what kind of dog wears a deerstalker hat?), he had in essence been your typical dog – panting, over-eager – and he was now a little less so. Interesting. Our acquaintance was causing us to change already.

A large paw passed in front of my field of vision, quickly followed by the sound of snapping paws.

"Huh?" I said, uncharacteristically struck dumb. I felt as though I was emerging from a trance.

"Earth to Catson," the dog said.

Is there anything more annoying than the old "Earth to X"?

"Earth to Catson," the dog said again, flicking his paw gently against my skull repeatedly in a tapping motion.

Apparently so. A skull-flick definitely beats "Earth to X" on the annoyance scale.

"I am, as always, present and accounted for," I said with no small degree of grumpiness.

"I don't know about that 'always' … " he started to say before I interrupted.

"Are you going to say something important soon, or are you simply going to go on insulting me? Because if it is to be the latter, I may as well go back to daydreaming."

"Dreaming of squirrels, were you?"

"I prefer not to say." Well, I certainly wasn't about to tell him that I'd actually been thinking of him.

"Fine, have it your way," he continued. "Finally, you will recall that the murderer, who I apprehended through the use of my superior detecting skills, was a rather tall man with tiny feet by the name of Jefferson Hope."

"I don't know as that I'd word it all quite like that, but yes, that is what happened."

"Good, because that brings us to –"

"Utah!" I cried triumphantly.

Two could play at this game.

CHAPTER ELEVEN

"Just about," the dog said. "I have a story to tell you first. Shall we repair to the drawing room?"

He meant the living room, of course. I'd learned rather early on in my acquaintance with him that he would never use one word for a thing if he could use a grander, more important-sounding one.

Whenever Bones settles down on the floor, it's always massively annoying. He either flops down wherever he's standing, with no regard to where he is or what he might knock over with that great big tail of his, or he adopts a trial-and-error approach – this spot here, that spot there – as if it's so hard to get it just right. He's a regular Goldilocks like that. Me, I'm so much simpler. I just find whatever spot is in line with the sun coming through the window, so my fur will feel warm and cozy, and I'm all set.

As I curled up before the fireplace, preparing to listen, I did wonder. I'd heard of drawing-room mysteries, of course. Hasn't everyone? But it had never occurred to me before that it could mean me in a drawing room listening to a dog tell me about a mystery.

"The story I am about to tell you," he started, draping an elbow over the mantelpiece, "begins a few decades ago … "

He had a way of speaking, drawing every word out, milking it for all the drama it was worth. I would have liked to walk away, show him I wasn't really interested in his story. There was just one problem: I totally was. Then:

Knock.

Knock. Knock.

Knock. Knock. Knock. Knock. Knock.

Who could it be?

For the first time it occurred to me. Despite Bones's overconfidence that clients would just somehow find us, could this be about a new case?

CHAPTER TWELVE

"I'll get it, Bosses, I'll get it!"

Mr. Javier came flying out of the kitchen, held aloft by his jetpack. Expertly, he flew down the long flight of stairs and pulled open the door.

Was there another murder afoot?

Or – perhaps even worse – could it be the dreaded Moriarty?

No. It was puppies.

I could tell this from the incessant yapping that is particular to the youth of the dog species. You'd never hear a group of kittens being so loud. Also because I heard Waggins say to Mr. Javier, in his

51

street-urchin accent: "Is Mr. Bones at home? Can he come out and play?"

"Your little friends are here," I said wryly.

"Yes, he is," I heard Mr. Javier say to Waggins. "But he and Dr. Catson are busy discussing important matters in the drawing room."

I collapsed my head into my paws. Great. Now the dog had the turtle calling the living room the drawing room too.

"That's quite all right, Mr. Javier!" Bones bellowed. "You may send the puppies up!"

There followed all the scampering and annoying displays of enthusiasm one would expect from a six-pack of puppies as they made their hurried way up into the drawing room. Er, I mean living room.

Behind them, a hovering Mr. Javier brought up the rear.

"Waggins!" Bones enthused. "And puppies!" This last confirmed something I'd been suspecting: that Bones had his own issues with names, meaning he had never bothered to learn what the other five were called, still had no clue, and now was too embarrassed to ask.

Before anyone could say anything further, the six-pack of puppies were falling all over themselves in their eagerness to greet their good friend, the dog. Big as he was, their sheer numbers soon brought him to the floor. Then commenced the kind of overenthusiastic canine display of affection that I hope to never see the likes of again – all that tumbling and rolling. At one point I had to actually shout, "Look out for that vase!" but no one was listening.

At last, the puppies exhausted by their exertions, order was somewhat restored.

"Now, you lot sit and behave," Waggins admonished the other five, as though *he* hadn't been involved. "You just sit there on the couch and listen to what Mr. Bones has to say."

Obediently, the puppies lined up in a military straight line side by side on the sofa, with Waggins all the way at one end and Bones sitting up importantly on the floor in front of them.

"I was just about to tell dear Dr. Catson," Bones said, "a story involving the last case we worked on.

You do remember, don't you, er, John Smith, the Secretary, and the double murder which culminated in the arrest of Jefferson Hope?"

The five unnamed puppies thumped their Cocker Spaniel tails and wagged their heads and Waggins said, "Remember it, sir? We helped you to solve it!"

"Just so," Bones said. "Would you like to hear the story as well, then?"

More eager tail thumping and head wagging. Oh, I did wish they would stop. If they kept it up, Bones would return to his overeager ways.

"Ahem."

Who said that?

"*Ahem. Ahem-ahem-ahem-ahem-AHEM!*"

"Oh!" Bones said. "Mr. Javier!"

"Why have all the puppies been invited to listen to the mystery story but not Mr. Javier?"

"Well, I – "

"Does Mr. Javier not like mystery stories? Is Mr. Javier not considered to be intelligent? *Do you think that Mr. Javier is just a housekeeper/cook without a brain in his head?*"

When did Mr. Javier become so testy? And when did the turtle begin referring to himself in the third person?

"Yes, well – " Bones tried again.

"Has Mr. Javier no feelings? Does Mr. Javier not bleed when you prick him?"

And now the turtle was quoting Shakespeare!

"Of course you are welcome to join us," Bones said graciously, recovering from his initial surprise at the turtle onslaught. "Please sit." With his paw, he indicated the one comfy seat not currently occupied by puppies. It just so happened to be the comfy cushion in the bay window, *my* usual favorite spot for napping.

I was forced to settle for one of the wing chairs. Since it was still facing the fireplace, and since I couldn't turn it around by myself, I was further forced once I was seated to crane my neck around the back of the chair so I could see the group. I suppose I could have taken a seat on the floor, like the dog, but I prefer not to floor-sit in polite company. Or impolite, for that matter – you know, puppies –

because company is still company.

"I just assumed," Bones said, continuing to placate the turtle, "that you were too busy with more important things to listen to my story."

"The dusting can wait," Mr. Javier said. "I would like to be entertained. I would like to be intellectually stimulated for once."

"Very well. Then I shall begin."

Finally! I thought.

"But it is quite a tale I am about to tell you," the dog said with his usual air of self-importance, as he gave stern looks all around but mostly at the puppies, "so I do hope there will be no interruptions."

The puppies smirked and snickered at this.

"Limited interruptions?" Bones tried, hopefully.

"HA!" Mr. Javier barked a most un-Mr.-Javier-like laugh. "We shall see about *that*."

CHAPTER THIRTEEN

"Once upon a time," the dog began, "or, in this instance, several decades ago ... "

"I hope this won't be too much like a history lesson," Waggins piped up. "I've never been much good with history."

"You should learn to be," Bones said, glaring at him, "but I assure you, it will not. As I was saying – "

"He's going to tell us all about Utah," I whispered to the puppies and Mr. Javier.

"Not geography!" Waggins cried, clapping a paw over his eyes.

"Not that either!" Bones assured him loudly. "Now will you all please just listen!"

We stared back at him, uniformly wounded. Well, he didn't need to shout at us, did he?

"Somewhere, in the United States of America, in the desert – " Bones attempted to begin again.

"Is it all desert over there," Puppy #1 asked, "in the United States of America?"

"Not at all," Bones said. "Some of it is desert, some of it contains mountains, and much of it borders on the ocean. In fact, it contains nearly every form of landscape and weather one could imagine."

He may have hated to be interrupted, but he equally loved being the one with all the knowledge. Which was annoying.

"You talk about it as though you have firsthand knowledge," I said testily, "like you've been there yourself."

"Oh, but I have, my dear Catson," he said, clearly surprised by my comment. "I'm a world traveler. I've been just about everywhere."

Well, lah-di-dah. A world traveler. This made me feel like Fred the horse. "Even Antarctica?" I said, accompanied by a snort.

"Of course," he said, amending, "well, in the summer."

I resented this, all of it. I'd never had occasion to travel very far from home. Even the Cat Wars were fought somewhat locally.

"In the desert of the United States of America, several decades ago, there was a man and a little girl," Bones said.

"How old was the little girl?" asked Puppy #2.

"About five, if memory serves," Bone said. "Now, this man and this little girl were not related, but they were, however, the sole survivors of a group that had originally numbered at least twenty."

"Were the rest of their company murdered?" asked Puppy #5, with an unseemly level of glee at such a prospect.

"Not at all," Bones said. "The rest were merely the victims of a variety of misfortunes that tended to befall travelers traveling west in those days."

"But *will* there be a murder in the story?" Puppy #5 pressed. "Like, really soon?"

"Perhaps," Bones said. "You must wait and listen."

CHAPTER FOURTEEN

"The man and the girl, as I said, were near death," Bones said.

"Did he say that part before?" Puppy #3 said.

"I don't think so," Puppy #4 said. "If he had, I'd surely have remembered."

"Bones," I said, "do you think we might have some names for the man and the girl? I think it will get confusing, calling them 'the man' and 'the girl,' if there are other men and girls in the story."

"Quite so, my dear Catson. For while there is just the one girl, there are as yet many men to come in the tale. We shall call the man … " Here he tapped his paw against his chin thoughtfully. "Joe Fur."

Fur. Now, there was a fabulous name!

I have a lot of fur myself, all over my body, and I am very fond of it.

"And the girl?" I prompted.

"Well, since there's only one of her in the story, I see no point – "

"Yes, but what if she grows up during the course of the tale? It will be odd calling her 'the girl' if she becomes an old woman at some point in the telling."

"Fine. We shall call her Lucy. Lucy Fur."

"And why does she have the same name as the man? They weren't related, right?"

"They weren't, but since all of her family died before the tale begins, the man, Joe Fur, claims her as his daughter." Bones sighed. "May I go on now?"

I stared at him blankly. "Who is trying to stop you?"

CHAPTER FIFTEEN

"As our scene opens," Bones said, "we find Joe Fur and Lucy Fur –although she is not known by that last name as yet, Catson – in the desert. They are near death, like so many have been before them. Suddenly!" And here he waved an arm in the air as if calling the vision in his mind into sight. "On the horizon, a thunderous cloud of dust approaches!"

"Will they die in a dust storm?" Puppy #2 asked, sounding fearful.

"That would be disappointing," said Puppy #5, exhibiting what I now suspected to be his *very* bloodthirsty nature. "I was hoping for a murder, possibly two, to kick things off."

"I'm afraid to disappoint you, my young friends," Bones said. "But at this juncture, there will be no deaths by dust or otherwise. Rather, the dust storm is the prelude to their salvation!"

"*Salvation?*" Puppy #5 made a face. "That doesn't sound like very much fun."

"Perhaps not for you," Bones said. "But for Joe Fur and Lucy, it is a wonderful thing. Coming towards them are ten *thousand* living people, some on horseback, some in wagons, and many on foot. There are men, women, and even children in their numbers."

"Did he say ten *thousand?*" Puppy #4 said, incredulous. "That would be like a whole town!"

"I did indeed say that," Bones said, "and it *was* like a whole town, as you so brilliantly put it."

Puppy #4 preened with pride. I doubted he had had anyone in his life to compliment him on his brain power before now.

"Because," Bones said, "these ten thousand were heading west for that very purpose: to start their very own town."

"But why?" Puppy #2 asked.

"Oh, I could list all sorts of reasons, all having to do with either politics or what-have-you."

Personally, I was curious about the what-have-you.

What can I say? Politics tends to bore me. Perhaps one day, if they ever allow a cat to hold elected office – Prime Minister Catson, perhaps? – I'll change my mind. But until then, give me what-have-you over politics any day.

Bones gave a dismissive wave of his hand. "That part really doesn't matter. For our purposes, it is enough to know that *their* purpose was to find their own little place in the world. I will tell you, though, that there are some people who believe that only people who think like them are right and that everyone else is wrong. The people heading toward Joe Fur and Lucy were those kinds of people. They all had like-minded beliefs on certain subjects and they only wanted to live among those who shared those beliefs."

"Kind of like their own private Utah," I said.

"More or less," Bones said.

"No, I mean really," I said. "We've finally arrived at Utah, haven't we?"

"Just about," Bones said. "Now, this group of ten thousand … I can't keep calling them 'this group of ten thousand.' It's becoming cumbersome. Nor do I want to use their real name, for I know some of you," and here he cast a glance at me, "have trouble with certain names from time to time. So we need to pick a new title for them."

I resented this.

"How about," Bones suggested, "if we simply refer to them as the Group?"

The puppies looked at each other, then at me. I looked back at the puppies before we heard a loud "Ahem!" Then the puppies all exchanged looks with Mr. Javier before Mr. Javier exchanged looks with me. I can safely say that by the time we were done exchanging looks, we were all dizzy from spinning our heads every which way.

Speaking for the room, I said, "Works for us."

"Splendid!" Bones said. "Now, back to my story. So, a thundering herd was approaching Joe Fur and Lucy!" Again with the arm gesture as though creating a real vision.

As he set the scene, describing the thundering hordes of people and animals coming Joe and Lucy Fur's way, he made it all seem so realistic that I saw Puppy #2 slip down from the sofa, slink around the edge of the room and leap up onto the comfy cushion in front of the bay window, curling up beside Mr. Javier for comfort. One wouldn't think that a hard-shelled reptile could function as a security blanket, but there you go.

"And who do you think was the man at the very front?" Bones asked.

Honestly. He expected us to guess? Right now? But we were all still so dizzy!

"Stangerson!" Bones cried triumphantly.

We all stared back at him blankly.

"Come on!" Bones cried, a little less triumphant now; a little more desperate. "You know who I'm talking about!"

We really didn't.

"*The Secretary!*"

CHAPTER SIXTEEN

Well, blow me down.

"The *Secretary*?" I gazed at Bones in open-mouthed shock. Typically, I don't like physically to appear foolish, but I was that shocked. "You mean to tell me," I said, "that the *Secretary*, the second murder victim in our last case, was the leader of these ten thousand people?"

"Well, technically, he was not the leader. There was actually another leader over everybody – and we'll get to that part shortly – but the lead horse of the ten thousand heading toward Joe Fur and Lucy? That was the Secretary. Well, actually, that wasn't him. It was his father."

"So," I said, still amazed, "you mean to tell me that the Secretary was not always the Secretary, but was once the son of a sort of leader of a group of people?"

"I am saying exactly that," Bones said.

"I know Dr. Catson's not done being amazed," Waggins piped up, "but could you continue with the tale anyway?"

"Of course," Bones said. "When the father of the Secretary and the Group came upon Joe Fur and Lucy, they offered to bring them along on their trip west and to feed them. The father of the Secretary even offered to have his wife care for Lucy beside his own children in their wagon, for the father of the Secretary had a family, while Joe Fur did not. The only demand the Group made on Joe Fur and Lucy, the only thing they asked, was that Joe and Lucy agree to think just like them."

"Is that all?" I snorted. "You can't demand that others think just like you do."

"Normally, I would wholeheartedly agree with

you on that, my dear Catson. Although, I do think the world would be a better place if everyone thought like me."

I snorted even louder, but the dog ignored me.

"I'm afraid, though," the dog said, "in this instance, I cannot agree, because that is exactly what happened."

CHAPTER SEVENTEEN

"That's right," Bones said, much to my astonishment. "Joe Fur and Lucy agreed to think just like the Group. Or, to put it more accurately, Joe agreed on both their behalf since a child Lucy's age wouldn't have been able to enter into such agreement with any amount of understanding."

"Is he trying to say that young'uns like us are stupid?" Puppy #3 said to Puppy #4.

"Not at all," Bones assured Puppy #3 before Puppy #4 could respond. "Only that a human child of age five could not be expected to understand the predicament the Furs found themselves in."

"Human children," I added, in Bones's defense, "are not as sophisticated as you lot."

I wasn't sure I necessarily believed as much, but the puppies looked so offended that anyone would think them stupid because of their age. Also, I supposed it didn't hurt *too* much, to back the dog every now and then.

"I'm glad we have that settled," Bones said. "Of course, we all know that kittens are not as smart as puppies either, and most certainly not if the puppy in question is me in my youth – "

What? And after I'd agreed with him!

" – but that is neither here nor there," Bones continued, "for I have another fun fact to share. I know I said the father of the Secretary was only the leader of the caravan of ten thousand, and that is true. But, remember I also said, there was another leader who was the head of everything and everybody, including the father of the Secretary."

"And who was that?" I said.

"Tell you what, my dear Catson. Why don't I make it easy on you: We'll just call him the Leader."

"Fine," I agreed, resignedly. By this point, I was through being offended, at least for the time being. I was overdue for a nap and a meal and just wanted to get to the heart of the story so that I could go get both.

I was in the midst of thinking about that happy prospect – a nap! – when I glimpsed something outside the window that put me on full wide-awake alert.

"Squirrel!" I shouted, pointing.

Every creature in the room raced to the bay window, crowding in around Mr. Javier and Puppy #2.

"Are you sure?" Bones cried. "Where did he go?"

"He was here just a moment ago," I said. "I saw him staring in the window with his beady little eyes. Do you think it could have been that Moriarty fellow, coming to spy on us?"

At the mention of Moriarty, the puppies cringed. Even Mr. Javier cringed. Did *everyone* know Moriarty?

"You must not give in to fear, my dear Catson," Bones said.

"I wasn't! I – "

"You must not begin seeing shadows – in this case, squirrel-shaped shadows – where none exist."

"It was no shadow! It was a real sq – "

"Just because Professor Moriarty is a squirrel," Bones said, "it does not logically follow that all squirrels are Professor Moriarty."

I opened my mouth, shut it again. Fine. Let him have it his way.

"Okay, fine," I said. "Let's say, just for the sake of argument, that I did see a squirrel outside the window. How did he get there? We are, after all, on the second story."

"Elementary." Bones smooshed his face against the window, no doubt leaving some slobber on the formerly pristine panes. "He must have walked along those eaves up there, shimmied down the drainpipe and then hopped over to this ledge, and ... Over there!"

"Where?" I said. "What are you looking at?"

The dog pointed. There, on the flat roof of the brick building across the road from where we all

73

were, a building quite similar in outward appearance to my own row house, stood a squirrel on the white gutter.

"Now, how did he get all the way over there?" I said.

"Must've run along the telephone wires between the buildings," Waggins said, pointing.

Despite the distance, I would swear on anything that the squirrel winked and gave a mocking little wave before scurrying out of sight.

"Moriarty!" Bones cried.

I refrained from saying "I told you so." Sometimes, it's enough to let events speak for themselves.

"Well," Bones said with a sigh, "we'll never catch him right now. Might as well return to our tale."

I resumed my place on one of the wing chairs and Bones resumed his place on the floor, but now all the puppies except #5 crowded around Mr. Javier for comfort. It was like he'd become their mascot or den mother. As for Puppy #5, he pulled out one of Bones's chew toys, facing off against it and attacking like it might be an enemy.

"So," Bones said, "to sum up, we have the Leader, who is at the top of everything. But right below him, there are four other men, who have almost as much power as he does. Of these four, one is the father of the Secretary and two don't figure into the story, at least not at this point. Now, can you guess the fourth?"

I groaned. "Guessing games, Bones? Seriously?"

"Think, Catson."

"But I'm so hungry!"

"I know you can guess this one, Catson. In fact, I'm sure of it. Really try. *Think*."

I thought.

I thought and I thought and I thought.

I thought of all the people he knew that I also knew, because it only made sense that it should be someone we both knew. Otherwise, why would he think that I knew what he knew?

It couldn't be Inspector Strange or Inspector No One Very Important – both of whom would be impossible choices for this, a high-ranking position in some group in the U.S., not to mention they'd have been too young back then – or Mr. Javier; several decades back, he'd have still been in Castile.

I strained and I strained, trying to think of who the most improbable person would be.

Then, I got it, snapping my paw at him several times in rapid succession and crying: "The other victim from the last case! The German! The one whose name I couldn't get right! You're talking about, er, John Smith!"

CHAPTER
EIGHTEEN

"Brava, Dr. Catson!" The dog actually clapped for me. "I knew you had it in you! Although, it was not, er, John Smith, but rather, his father. Now, give the cat a cookie, Mr. Javier. Come to think of it, it's time we all had a meal."

While the others debated what to get – they were sure they wanted "the takeout," as Mr. Javier likes to put it, but they weren't sure which kind – I marveled at the craziness of what I'd just learned.

"But how is such a thing possible?" I shouted to Bones over the clatter of the puppies, who were busily passing back and forth takeout menus amongst themselves; I could only guess that most of their meals came from leavings in the streets or trash bins behind the city's restaurants, as opposed to a choice between Lebanese and Chinese. "Both the father of the Secretary *and* the father of, er, John Smith, our two victims in the last case, were somehow involved together previously, were in fact two of four sub-leaders in some sort of group … in *Utah*?"

"How many times have I told you, my dear Catson, that once you have removed the impossible, whatever remains – however improbable – must be the truth?"

"None," I said dryly. "I'm quite certain I've never heard that one before in my life."

"Then I am telling you now."

I looked over at Mr. Javier. The turtle was having a devil of a time trying to get the puppies to all agree on just one place to get their dinners from. In the end, they could not agree, so it was decided that we would order spaghetti and meatballs from the Italian place on First Street, chicken lo mein from the Chinese place on Second Street, and several nice juicy steaks from Samuel's Steakhouse on Third Street. We had explained to the puppies that anything to do with seafood was no longer an option, a conversation that went something like:

Puppy #1: I've always wanted to try lobster.

Mr. Javier: Lobsters are my friends.

Puppy #2: Maybe some shrimp then?

Mr. Javier: The shrimps are my friends.

Waggins: Clams? Mussels? Oysters? Salmon? Or maybe –

Mr. Javier: Am I not making myself sufficiently clear here? *All* the creatures of the sea are my friends! Nay, they are like my family. So asking me to –

And there he proceeded with a long speech about how all the creatures of the sea were his brethren and then it took a most gruesome turn when he went into detail about what life would be like if he expected us to order takeout food comprised of our own species. Puppy #5 didn't seem to mind too much – as far as he's concerned, the more gruesome a thing is, the better – but the rest of us did see Mr. Javier's point. So, like I said: spaghetti etcetera.

Of course, the added guests for dinner meant

moving several heavy chairs from their usual positions against the wall up closer to the dining room table. Before the jetpack, such an operation might have taken Mr. Javier a whole day. Not because the chairs were so heavy – the little turtle is surprisingly strong – but because of the slowness factor. Now, however, he had the task accomplished in a trice. And in another trice, he had jetted all over town, returning with our various suppers.

While Mr. Javier was gone, and while the dog and puppies made wide use of the chew toys, I made use of my own telephone. It's not a device I normally care to use myself, but I'd had a thought earlier in the day, now I had means and opportunity to do something about that thought, and so I did. The others were so busy chewing, that even the dog – with his so-called superior powers of observation – didn't notice what I was doing.

Like I said, the turtle was quick. Within an hour we were all seated around the table, dishing up food. Even Mr. Javier sat with us. The turtle was determined not to miss any of the story.

As I lifted a forkful of spaghetti toward my mouth, I thought how, the few times the public human detectives had been in our presence while Bones and I ate, they'd marveled at the sight of a cat using a fork properly. For some reason, the dog utilizing utensils didn't throw them half so much — perhaps because the dog never used them properly.

This reaction always caused me to laugh silently to myself. Seriously? Once they accepted that animals could talk, this was what they stumbled over?

"Now that everyone has food on their plates," the dog announced from his head of the table, "I shall continue. Let's fast forward twelve years in our story."

"Why?" I said. "Did nothing of significance happen in those twelve years?"

"Not really," Bones said, "unless you include Joe Fur doing very well for himself and Lucy Fur growing up and reaching the age of seventeen. In fact, Joe Fur did so well for himself, he grew to be quite wealthy and a well-respected member of the Group. There was just one problem."

"Which was?" I prompted.

"Joe Fur had yet to get married and this was frowned upon by the Group, for the Group believed in marriage, very much so."

"Well," said Puppy #5, "I for one am glad he didn't get married. Marriage, to me, means there might be a romance in the story, which would be worse than history or geography, and the exact opposite of mystery."

"I think," Bones said carefully, "that you are quite wrong about romance, but no, this is not a romance. Or at least, not for very long."

Whatever could he mean by that?

"If Joe Fur would not get married," Bones said, "who do you think, in his household, the Group would want to see married?"

This was so easy, even the puppies could do the math. Subtract Joe Fur, and who was left in his household?

"Lucy Fur?" Puppy #4 gasped. "The Group wanted Lucy Fur to get married ... to one of them?"

"That is precisely what they wanted, my young friend," Bones said. "The only problem was that was *not* what they got."

CHAPTER
NINETEEN

There he went with the cliffhangers again.

"Then who?" I asked, exasperated. "Who did they get instead?"

"All in good time, my dear Catson, all in good time. First, I must tell you a story."

"I thought that's what you *were* doing!" I said, more exasperated still. *Honestly*.

"I suppose I am," the dog said. "Very well. A story within the story, then."

Oh, brother.

My heavy sighs, my exaggerated eye rolls – they did nothing to affect or deter the dog.

"Picture this," he said, squinting at a dusty horizon only he could see. "Young Lucy Fur at age seventeen, still considered young to us for a human, but in that time and place considered to be a young woman of marriageable age. One day, she is out riding on a horse – "

"She has a *horse* now?" Puppy #1 interjected. "When did she get a *horse*?"

Bone chose to ignore him – a rare move on his part. Some animals and humans are just always getting distracted. True, I can get distracted by a moving piece of yarn, but that, I think we can all agree, is completely understandable.

"No matter. So, Lucy was out riding around on her horse when, suddenly, she found herself trapped inside a herd of cattle."

"How does that even happen?" Puppy #2 asked. "Did she not see them coming? Could she not get out of the way?"

Wisely, with a heavy sigh and a paw swipe across his own brow, Bones chose to ignore these questions too. "It seems to me," Puppy #3 said, "that lots of things happen suddenly in the west in the United States of America. Dust storms, herds of cattle surrounding you, even stories jumping ahead twelve years – it all happens suddenly."

"She was in dire peril! Then, suddenly!" Bones cried so loudly, I dropped my fork. "A man on a horse appears! Out of nowhere!"

"What did I tell you?" Puppy #3 said with a nudge to Puppy #4.

"The man saves Lucy!" Bones cried, louder yet.

For one who was normally such a practical being, the dog was certainly wrapped up in the romance of the thing.

"Afterward," Bones continued, in a less dramatic voice, "the man tells Lucy he believes that, years ago, his family and Lucy's family – or at least Joe Fur – knew each other in a different state within the United States of America. The man is just passing through, a stranger to the town when he rescued Lucy – and this is not the sort of town that likes strangers – but he decides to stick around for a bit. He finds a place to stay at an inn in town. He even makes a few friends – perhaps it's more accurate to call them acquaintances, since no one in the Group much cares for outsiders."

"But where did he even come from?" I said. "Did he really just appear out of nowhere?"

"Pretty much." The dog shrugged. "In those days, in the American West, people were always appearing out of nowhere. He was heading west, like so many before him, in hopes of finding gold."

"He had no money of his own?" I asked.

"Oh, he did." The dog shrugged again. "A fair amount, actually. But you know humans. They always want more."

That's certainly true.

"The man never made it far enough west to find gold, however," Bones said. "But he found something even better. He found love."

By this point, there were a few misty eyes in the room and Puppy #2 clasped his paws to his chest.

"To continue," Bones continued, "in time, the man falls in love with Lucy. Joe Fur really likes the man. The man wants to marry Lucy. Then the man says he must leave for two months."

"Wait. What?" I made my paw-to-paw timeout sign. "The man falls in love with her, says he wants to marry her … and then disappears for two months?"

"What can I say?" The dog shrugged. "Things were hard back then, in the west. That's the way it was, with people often having to go to other places to do things for a time."

He took another helping of spaghetti before continuing. "Of course, Joe Fur was thrilled with this turn of events. The last thing he wanted was for Lucy, who he really did think of as his daughter at this point, to marry anyone from the Group."

"But why?" Waggins said. "Seems to me, the Group done all right by old Joe Fur. They saved him from death. Gave him new people. Next thing you know, he's not only alive but wealthy too."

"Let's just say he had his reasons," Bones said, giving a most unsatisfactory answer to what seemed to me a perfectly logical question. "Let's just say that Joe Fur was very happy at the idea of Lucy marrying someone from outside the Group."

"Fine," I said, "let's just say that. And … ?"

"And," the dog said, "at this time, there were a group of people who … took care of things … whenever anyone tried to go outside the Group. And, also at this time, the Leader – you do all remember him, don't you?"

Plenty of nods all around.

"Yes, well, the Leader decided to pay Joe Fur a visit. He told him there'd been much talk among the sub-leaders of the Group and it had been decided that Lucy Fur should marry either, er, John Smith or the Secretary, both of them being sons of the sub-leaders and all grown up now."

"They decided?" I sputtered, sputtering a considerable amount of spaghetti out of my mouth. "Who were these *men* to decide who Lucy Fur should marry?"

"My dear Catson," Bones said, a rare look of sadness combined with sympathy on his face, "I do empathize with your feelings on this matter. But this is how it was at this time and place and with these people. This is what the Leader and the others wanted for Lucy. The Leader gave Joe Fur one month to decide: Would his daughter marry the man who was an outsider to the Group and suffer the consequences or marry one of the two chosen for her *by* the Group?"

"Seems like no choice at all," I said. "She should choose the one she wants."

"And I would agree with you," Bones said, "only keep in mind: I did tell you there was another group, whose job it was to take care of business for the Group, and this group within the Group was a very bad group indeed. Still, Joe Fur wanted what was best for his child. He did not want, er, John Smith for her. He did not want the Secretary for her. And so, he sent a telegram to the man who'd fallen in love with Lucy, a telegram calling him back."

I had a tear in my eye. I couldn't help it – the story was that romantic. Either that, or Mr. Javier had neglected to dust the chandelier in the dining room and my allergies were kicking up.

Then something struck me.

"You keep using 'the man' in place of the name for

this person Lucy Fur fell in love with," I said. "And yet, earlier, you said we were going to have some sort of names for the people in this story." I narrowed my eyes at him. "Just who is this 'the man'?"

"That is most observant of you, my dear Catson," the dog said, his own eyes twinkling. "Not only that, but you have hit on the most fun and intriguing part of the story. Who do *you* think the man is?"

"Oh no," I groaned, "not this again. Another guessing game?"

"*No.*" The dog's eyes flashed. "I don't want you to *guess*. I want you to use your deductive powers of reasoning. *Think*, Catson."

I went through the same process I had before, going through the list of people that the dog knew that I also knew, eliminating people based on impossibilities.

Once I finished, I did it all over again, because it couldn't possibly be possible, the person I thought it must be … could it?

"No!" I said.

"*Yes*," Bones said.

"But it can't be," I said.

"Oh, but it *is*," the dog said. "Come on, Catson, say it."

"Jefferson Hope?"

Slowly, the dog nodded.

"But it can't be," I said again, dumbfounded. "The man who is 'the man,' the man who fell in love with Lucy and she with him, is *the* Jefferson Hope, the man responsible for the deaths of, er, John Smith and the Secretary?" I paused. "*That* Jefferson Hope?"

"Ding, ding, ding!" the dog cried, triumphant.

CHAPTER
TWENTY

Even though I was the one who put it all together, I still couldn't believe it, even with Bones's cheery and congratulatory "Ding! Ding! Ding!"

"But how is that possible?" I said. "You mean to tell me that Jefferson Hope wasn't always a murderer, but rather was once a young man in love?"

"And why should that surprise you so, my dear Catson? We are all changing all the time. None of us end up exactly as we have begun, not unless we are to remain babies or puppies or kittens all of our lives."

"Or hatchlings," Mr. Javier put in, somewhat angrily.

"Pardon me?" said Bones.

"Hatchlings," Mr. Javier said. "You named all the others but you did not mention baby turtles. When we turtles are babies, we are called hatchlings."

"Ah, yes!" Bones said. "And thank you so much for correcting me!"

Even though Bones normally hated to be corrected, he thanked Mr. Javier with such a soothing voice, I could only guess that he had no desire to raise the turtle's ire further. Well, who could blame him?

"And thank you also, Mr. Javier," Bones continued, indicating the remains of our supper, "for gathering this amazing spread for us. I cannot imagine that anyone in the land negotiates the intricacies of ordering and then collecting takeout with the same extraordinary skills that you exhibit."

OK, that was laying it on a bit thick. Surely, the turtle would see through this and realize the dog was only trying to stay on his good side?

And yet, the turtle didn't. Rather, he gave a slight bow of his reptile head in a display of humble pride.

Oh, brother. If Bones kept this up, the turtle would grow so full of himself, he'd be expecting all sorts of praise on a regular basis. Never mind praise, he'd probably demand a raise!

"Good," Bones said, "now that everyone is happy again, I shall continue with the story of our young man in love, the man we all know as Jefferson Hope."

"That's an excellent idea, Boss," Mr. Javier said, back to his usual pleasingly eager self. "But first, why don't you all retreat to the drawing room and I'll bring in dessert."

"What are we having?" I asked casually, as if this idea didn't appeal to me greatly. I must confess: I do have a sweet tooth.

"A new recipe I made this morning," Mr. Javier said, more eager still. "It's a pineapple upside-down cake. Something went a little wrong in the preparation, so instead it is a pineapple right-side-*up* cake, but I'm almost certain it will be good just the same."

CHAPTER TWENTY-ONE

Sometimes, the best cliffhanger one can come up with is a dessert coming out the opposite of the way it should. Despite that, Mr. Javier was right: His right-side-up pineapple upside-down cake was delicious if not what one would ever expect from an upside-down cake. And yet, I realized as I pawed up the last crumbs, weren't mysteries and even life itself like that too? You go into a thing expecting one thing and you wind up getting something else entirely. That sentence I just wrote – in some ways, it expresses perfectly my whole relationship with Bones.

"And back to our story," Bones said. "When last we left it, Joe Fur, having been told by the Leader that he had one month, thirty days, to decide who Lucy Fur would marry, had sent a message to Jefferson Hope calling for him to come back. A very interesting thing happened next."

He paused.

We waited.

"I hope," I said, "you're not expecting us to guess what that interesting thing was."

"Not at all," the dog said, forking up a mouthful of cake. "I was simply reflecting on how good this cake is and how glad I am that it does not contain chocolate, for that might kill me." He shrugged. "And the puppies." He set the plate aside. "In any event, Joe Fur returned home the next day to find two young gentlemen – and I use that word loosely – waiting for him inside."

"Had Hope returned so quickly?" Waggins asked. "Was he some kind of magician?"

"Neither," Bones said. "Besides, I did say there were two young men, did I not?"

97

"I suppose they couldn't have both been him," Waggins said, disappointed.

Thankfully, Bones chose not to respond to this idiotic comment. Instead, he said, "The two young gentlemen were – of course – the Secretary and, er, John Smith."

"What did those two want?" asked Puppy #5. "Does it have anything to do with murder?"

"Not quite," Bones said. "They wanted to make their individual cases as to why each of them respectively should be the one to marry Lucy Fur."

"Like she's some sort of prize?" I was outraged at this. "Like she herself should have no say in who she marries?"

"My dear Catson," Bones said, "that is *exactly* what Joe Fur said to them when they arrived. Furthermore, he told them that who Lucy married should be entirely up to her and that neither of them should return until and unless she called for one of them specifically."

"*Well*," I harrumphed, satisfied, "I should think so."

"There's just one problem," Bones said.

"Hmm?" from me.

"Joe Fur's method of dealing with things?" Bones gave a grim nod at his own words. "It had disastrous results."

CHAPTER TWENTY-TWO

"The two young gentlemen left angrily," Bones continued, jumping down and heading for the living room, before anyone could ask what he had meant by "disastrous results." The rest of us followed. "It is not always wise to provoke bad people, for it is impossible to guess what they might do with their anger."

"And what did they do?" asked Puppy #4, breathlessly from the position he had taken on the floor.

By this point, any idea of the military seating of the puppies lined up with backs straight on the

100

couch had completely deteriorated. Now they were all on the floor with Bones, so wrapped up in his story that their heads were propped up on paws as they clustered together in a comfortable puppy pile. They were like human children listening to a parent at bedtime – I've read of such things. Next, they'd be expecting Mr. Javier to serve them cookies and milk to go with the tale. But Mr. Javier wouldn't be doing that. He was too busy pretending to dust as he listened raptly to the story too. And since he was pretending to be busy, I was able to take back my comfy window seat. Although it felt somewhat less comfy now that I felt as though a squirrel of questionable character might be peeking in at me at any moment. The very idea made my hair stand slightly on end.

"Initially?" The dog shrugged. "Nothing. In the immediate aftermath of their departure, Joe Fur and Lucy were left to wait, hoping for the man she really loved to return in time."

Something struck me. "They were hoping for Hope," I said with wonder.

"Just so, Catson," Bones said. "They were hoping for Hope! Sadly, hope did not bring Hope that day or that night. Instead, the next morning, having had to go to sleep at some point, Joe Fur woke to find that a note written in the Leader's hand had somehow found its way into his home."

He paused.

I hoped he wasn't going to ask me the contents of the note. Sure, I had already guessed the identities of a couple of the people in his story, but I couldn't guess the contents of an entire note, much less one written decades before!

But no, the dog was merely milking the drama, completing the air of urgency as he leaned forward to say:

"The note *said*, in essence, that Joe Fur must comply with the wishes of the Group … *or else* … "

CHAPTER TWENTY-THREE

"Or else what?" Puppy #3 cried urgently. "Or else what?"

"That is the point, is it not?" Bones said coolly, relaxing backward on his haunches. After his cliffhanging "or else," he had sauntered over to one of the wing chairs, turned it to face the room, and leapt up on it.

"What point?" I said, exasperated. "What point could you possibly be going on about?"

"Is there anything worse," the dog said, looking quite satisfied with himself, "than a vague, open-ended 'or else'? Is there anything more ominous than the blank space following an 'or else,' a space that the mind can only fill with all manner of horrible guesses based on fear?"

Well, when he put it like that …

"I can think of worse things!" Mr. Javier piped up, raising a turtle arm in the air to call for attention.

"You *can*?" the dog said, incredulous. Then he waited.

"I only said I 'can,'" the turtle said, looking embarrassed, "meaning that I am sure I have the potential. I did not say that I am actually thinking of anything specific right this minute."

"That is quite all right," Bones said, "because I can."

"*You* can?" I said. "Then why did you rhetorically ask *us*? Now look what you've done. You've confused and upset Mr. Javier!"

"He'll get over it," the dog said, reverting back to his usual dismissive ways when it came to anyone else's feelings; or, really, feelings at all.

"The thing is," Bones continued, "there *was* a worse thing!"

I stared back at him. Well, I certainly wasn't about to give him a verbal prompt, not after he'd upset the turtle.

Actually, the turtle looked perfectly fine. Sometimes I like to at least try to rein the dog in so he doesn't get too carried away thinking he can run roughshod over everybody.

"As bad as that 'or else' was," the dog said, "poor Joe Fur was left to wonder: how did the note get inside his home? Someone must have been there while he slept. And if someone, or some *ones*, could get in once while he slept, was it not possible that it could happen again?"

The puppies, Mr. Javier and even I squirmed at this. What an awful thought!

An even more horrible thought occurred to me. Earlier, the squirrel had appeared on the ledge outside my bay window. That had been bad enough. But what if one day he were to gain entry? What if one day, at night, while I was sleeping, Professor Moriarty broke in here and –

"You're doing it again, aren't you?" Bones said.

"Hmm?" I said.

"You're thinking of squirrels," he said.

I nodded.

"Specifically," he said, "you're thinking of Professor Moriarty."

I nodded, more vehemently this time.

"Well, cut it out," he said.

Then he turned to the others, continuing with his tale as though he'd never interrupted it to talk to me about the squirrel.

"And as bad as all of *that* was," Bones said, "there was still worse to come. In addition to the threatening words, the note bore the number ... *29*."

Wait. What?

"After all of this," I said, confused, "receiving a threatening note, an ominous 'or else,' the idea of someone sneaking into your home while you sleep – how can a simple number be *still worse*?"

"Oh, but it was!" Bones said. "Why, it is all elementary. Do you not remember me saying that the Leader had given Joe Fur one month – 30 days – to decide whom Lucy should marry?"

"Of course I remember!" Then: "You mean … "

"Yes. The clock was already ticking. The Leader was informing Joe Fur that he now had a mere 29 days left, or else. Even worse than that – "

"Worse!"

"Each day thereafter, another slip of paper would appear, only these slips of paper no longer contained words, just the numbers in decreasing order, one decrease per day: 28, 27, 26, *25* – "

"Stop!" I cried, covering my ears with my paws. I couldn't stop imagining how horrible those notes must have been for Joe Fur and Lucy.

But even through my paws, I could hear Bones say, "That's right, it was awful for the Furs. Soon, there were just two days left. But here is a wonderful thing: They still hoped for Hope."

"They didn't give up hope!" I said, happy on their behalf.

"They did not," Bones said, "which is why it was doubly wonderful when, with just those two days left, Jefferson Hope returned."

"Hope has arrived!" I said.

"He did!" Bones said. "And then he and Joe Fur made their plans to escape with Lucy before time ran out. They snuck out that very night, taking only what was necessary. At one point they hid in the shadows, overhearing two members of the Group talking – obviously about them; stuff about needing to keep a close lookout lest Lucy escape – and ending their conversation with a cryptic password. It meant nothing to our hopeful travelers. It did, however, come in handy when, almost safely away, they came across a sentry on the outskirts of town. They were able to get away by employing this cryptic password."

He stopped abruptly there.

"So, they escaped!" I said, clapping my paws. "What a happy, Hope-y ending!"

"Well," the dog added dryly, "not exactly."

CHAPTER TWENTY-FOUR

I didn't even want to think about what he meant by "not exactly."

But it didn't matter what I wanted. Like a pineapple upside-down cake somehow coming out right-side up, it seemed that whatever I wanted Bones to do, he was sure to do the exact opposite.

"Having escaped the Group," Bones said, "or so they thought, Joe Fur and Lucy – accompanied by Jefferson Hope – were soon on the move. When there was no evidence of anyone trailing them by the next morning, the Furs gave sighs of relief and began to relax. Jefferson Hope, however, was not the sighing or relaxing sort. He urged them to move faster, to put more time and distance between themselves and the Group."

Bones sighed here.

"There are times when I think," he said, "if only they knew what people know now, that they can talk to animals. If only they could have talked to the horses, like I can … "

"Talk to the horses?" I snorted. "Like that would ever do anyone any good!"

"You know, Catson," he said, considering, "someday, you will have to overcome all your prejudices – "

"I?"

"And when you do, you will learn that there is always something to gain through peaceable conversation with other creatures."

"And what could have been gained in this instance by 'peaceable conversation with other creatures,' pray tell?"

"If the humans could have talked to their horses, perhaps they would have learned that their horses had been talking to other horses. That information, if followed, could have saved so many people so much heartache."

I opened my mouth. I shut my mouth. I can't say my opinion of horses had improved very much, but I couldn't fault his logic.

"Moving on," Bones said, "our little party of three did gain more distance between themselves and the Group. And with that increased distance came greater relief." Bones sighed again. "If only they knew … "

If only they knew … ? That was just as bad as "*or so they thought!*" Does any good ever come following either phrase? If you ask me, it's even worse than *or else* … At least with *or else*, there's always the possibility of a positive outcome, however slim, as long as one party gives in to the other party and does whatever the *or else* was put there for in the first place. But *if only they knew* and *or so they thought* – those phrases never bode well, the words their very selves indicating that misfortune is soon to call.

Having originally thought all this to myself, I

then spoke it all out loud, to which the dog replied:

"It never occurred to me before that you gave such philosophical matters so much thought."

I glared at him. Just how many insults had he shot at me with that single sentence?

"Then what happened?" Waggins asked. What, did the puppy not want to see a cat-and-dog fight?

"Thinking that they were relatively safe for the time being," Bones said, "Jefferson Hope took leave of the others. You see, their supplies were running low and he was the most capable among them to hunt for food. After all, if Joe Fur had been any good at that, he and Lucy would not have nearly starved to death in the desert, so many years ago."

"You say hunting," Mr. Javier said. "I hope it is not fish that we are about to see Mr. Jefferson Hope hunt."

"I can safely assure you," Bones said, "it was not fish. He had a rifle with him and no one uses a rifle on fish unless those fish are in a barrel."

This was possibly the most inaccurate thing I had ever heard the dog utter, but the turtle seemed satisfied, so I let it pass.

"It took a long time for Jefferson Hope to find what he was seeking," Bones said, "which, in a way, you could say was also the story of his life. By the time he finally returned several hours later, to the campsite where he'd left Joe Fur and Lucy earlier in the day, do you know what he found there?"

We stared back at him. How should we know?

"*Nothing*," Bones said. "He found *nothing*."

CHAPTER TWENTY-FIVE

"*Nothing?*" I half-shrieked at the dog. "How could he have found *nothing?* The mountains, the trees, the stones, the shrubbery, the very earth itself: did it all just – poof! – disappear?"

"Fine," he said, clearly annoyed at my exactness. "Of course, he found all those things you just mentioned and more, no doubt. But he didn't find three *horses.* He didn't find two *people.* He didn't find *Lucy.*"

"So, what?" Puppy #4 said dumbly. "Did they go poof?"

"Of course not!" said the dog. "Listen, and you shall learn!"

Could he not see, we *were* listening?

"As I said," the dog said, "Jefferson Hope did not find any traces of his own party. But he did find traces."

"Of?" I prompted.

"Many other horses' hoof prints, perhaps too many to count, not to mention many different men's footprints. They were leading up to the campsite from the direction of the Group and there were clearly just as many traveling in the direction from whence they had just come – back toward where the Group had settled."

"So, many people from the Group had been there?" I asked.

"Yes," he said, "but that was nowhere near the worst part."

I'm not going to ask, I'm not going to ask, I told myself. But then, I couldn't help it.

"And what *was* the worst part?" I demanded to know, on my behalf, on all our behalves.

"Searching the area more closely, poor Jefferson Hope came across a mound of freshly turned earth –

a grave, if you will."

Oh, this was bad. Still:

"Poor Jefferson Hope?" True, even I'd been pulled along by the tale of young Jefferson Hope in love, but: "Should we really be feeling bad for the man we know to be a double murderer?"

"But he wasn't that then, was he?" Bones said. "Imagine him, finding the grave, wondering if the woman he loved lay beneath it. Of course, as it turned out, she didn't, but it was nearly as bad."

"How nearly?" I asked warily.

"No sooner had he found the grave, than Jefferson Hope spied a piece of paper on a stick, sticking out of the ground as sticks stuck in the ground are wont to do. On that flimsy piece of paper was the name Joe Fur accompanied by that day's date, the day of his death."

"The Group killed Joe Fur?" I said, shocked.

"Someone did," Bones said. "With Lucy gone and all the evidence before him, Jefferson Hope could only conclude that the Group, having killed her father, had then seized Lucy Fur, with the intent to bring her back to wed either the Secretary or, er, John Smith."

"The scoundrels!" I said, clenching my paws tightly.

"I must agree with you there," Bones said. "No doubt, Jefferson Hope shared that sentiment, which is why – right then and there – he vowed to take his revenge."

CHAPTER TWENTY-SIX

"Revenge," I echoed. "I recall that in the first case we worked together, when we found the body of, er, John Smith, someone had written on the wall in blood the word 'RACHE'. The public human detectives assumed it was the partially written name of a woman, Rachel, but you said it was in fact the German word for 'revenge'."

"How wise of you to remember," Bones said.

I took the compliment in stride with a slight bow, neglecting to add that it was all fresh in my memory because I'd written of all this in *Case File #1: Doggone*, which I didn't want him to know because who knew what he'd think if he did? Probably the most he'd do was criticize me for not making him appear even smarter, but why take that chance? In all likelihood, he'd just be so flattered to discover me writing about him in books, it would go to his head. His head was so big already. Did it really need another reason to grow any bigger?

"So," Bones said, "as I said, Jefferson Hope set out for revenge. First, though, there was the small matter of even getting back to the Group. With his own horse gone too, he had no choice but to set off on foot. And, while it had taken him just a little over a day on horseback to arrive at his present location, it now took him several days on foot to return to where he'd been."

"Isn't it always just like that?" Waggins said, with a rueful wag of his head. "I always find that the journey out to a place is always faster and better than the journey back."

Who knew the puppy was such a philosopher? No wonder he was leader of the pack. It might not have been much as observations go but it was pretty impressive coming from a puppy.

"After several days of journeying," Bones said, "having drawn close to where the Group resided, Jefferson Hope came across a man. Although Jefferson Hope had never been particularly friendly with anyone from the Group outside of the Furs – Jefferson Hope was an outsider and the Group was decidedly unfriendly to outsiders – as I said before, during his time at the inn he had made a few acquaintances and this man was one of those. In fact, he was closer to this man than any of the others."

"Name, please?" I prompted.

But the dog just waved a dismissive paw. "In this instance, the name of the man does not matter. In this instance, the man will only be with us for this very short part of the story and then he shall disappear from it entirely."

"Fine," I grumbled. "Go ahead then. Just keep referring to him as 'the man' if you want to."

"Thank you, I shall. Although the man was clearly terrified at the risk of being seen with Jefferson Hope,

Jefferson Hope prevailed upon him to tell him what had happed to Lucy Fur, and that is when he learned of her fate."

"What happened? What happened?" more than one voice cried out.

"Why, she had been married, of course," the dog said. "Only just the day before, while Jefferson Hope had been hurrying to reach her, she'd been married."

"To who?" we cried, some of us more correctly amending that to "To whom?"

"Why to, er, John Smith of course."

CHAPTER TWENTY-SEVEN

"No!" I reeled back in horror.

To their credit, the puppies and Mr. Javier reeled back in horror too.

"Oh, yes," Bones said. "I wish I could tell you a different story but I fear I cannot."

"So then," I said, "Jefferson Hope was too late?"

Too late! Oh, the tragedy of too late!

"Well, for that, he was," Bones said. "The man told Jefferson Hope that both the Secretary and, er, John Smith had been part of the large group within the Group that had trailed Jefferson Hope and the Furs into the mountains. He further said that upon

122

returning to the Group with Lucy, there had been quite a fight over who should then get to marry her."

"My," I said, "for a man who hasn't even been given a name, he said an awful lot."

"Indeed, he did," Bones said, wholly missing my sarcastic tone. "The man *further* said that it was the Secretary who had killed Joe Fur and that he thought that – somehow! – this meant he had a greater claim to marry Lucy, but the Leader ended up giving her to, er, John Smith."

"*Gave* her?" I did not even know this Lucy Fur, but it galled me to think of men fighting over her in such a way, giving her no choice in where she would go, or whom she would go there with.

"I do realize that empathy has never been my strong suit," the dog said, showing rare self-insight, "but in this instance, I can empathize wholly. No being or animal should be treated in such a fashion."

"How did she react to it?" I asked.

"I'm afraid there was no fight left in her. The man told Jefferson Hope that when she was brought back to the Group, she looked close to death. And, in fact, she was dead within thirty days."

That last thing Bones said was so awful, it hurt me to even write it down. But it is what he said. And, worse was to come.

"As it turned out," he said, "er, John Smith was not upset by her passing at all. As it turned out, he'd only ever wanted to marry her so he could get his hands on her wealthy father's property."

That was what was worse.

After a sad sigh, ever practical, Bones continued on with, "But there is nothing to be done about that now, so let us not dwell upon that part. Let us turn our attention back to Jefferson Hope, who had vowed his revenge."

Funny, before this day, I'd thought of Jefferson Hope with the same scorn I would give any common villain. Now, I almost pitied the man.

"Over the next months and years, Jefferson Hope made many attempts to exact his revenge – and the Secretary and, er, John Smith made similar attempts to remove him from the picture before he could remove them – but it was all to no avail, on all of their parts. At last, having run near out of money, Jefferson Hope gave up and left, going yet further west to remake his fortune."

"Only he didn't give up," I said.

"That," Bones said, "he did not."

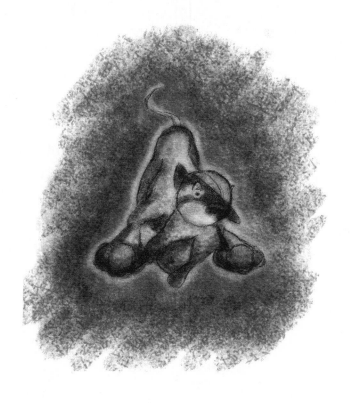

CHAPTER TWENTY-EIGHT

"Years later," Bones said, "having finally remade his fortune, Jefferson Hope returned to the area where the Group had been only to find that, while most of the Group were still there, the Secretary and, er, John Smith were no longer among them. For whatever reasons, the Secretary and, er, John Smith had chosen to leave the Group. And so, like Jefferson Hope himself, they were now considered by the Group to be outsiders."

"So then what happened?" I asked.

"By this time," Bones said, "er, John Smith was still a very wealthy man – he did still have Joe Fur's money, after all – but things had not gone as well for the Secretary, who had far less money."

"Ah!" I said, understanding finally clicking in. "So that is how he became the Secretary."

"Just so," Bones said. "At any rate, now armed with his own fresh and large supply of cash, Jefferson Hope dogged the traces of the two villains, like a dog with a bone."

"Only the two?" Waggins said. "But there were other men involved in the kidnapping of the Furs. I mean, when you think about it, the whole entire Group was responsible, in one way or another, for what happened to Lucy and her adopted father."

"But that's just it," I said. "Earlier, Bones said the Group numbered ten thousand. Even a man as determined as Jefferson Hope couldn't hope to avenge himself on ten thousand. He could, however, do so with the two men he blamed most."

"Precisely," Bones said. "Your deductive powers are increasing by the day, Catson."

Kiss him. Kill him. It's always fifty-fifty.

"Jefferson Hope tracked all over the United States

of America. Anytime he would draw close, though, somehow they would get wind of him and get away. He then traced them from the States to Europe, and across that continent from country to country until he found them finally – finally! – here in England."

We all stared at him, waiting for him to continue. While we stared at him, he pulled out his pipe and played with it; he never smokes the thing, thankfully, for it is a filthy habit. Then he studied his manicure … all four paws. For good measure, he pretended to box and fence his way across the living room even though he hadn't bothered to get out either his gloves or sword. He *even* picked up and began to play a song on his violin. But no amount of staring appeared to induce him to speak again.

Therefore, I was forced to say:

"*And?*"

"And what?" He appeared perplexed, stopping his bow mid-strum.

"And what else happened?"

"You know what happened, my dear Catson." He set his violin down, resumed his seat. "It happened at the beginning of our last case which is somehow now part of this case too."

"Yes but – " I started to object, but from the look on his face I realized there was little point. He'd said as much as he would for now. If there was more, it would come later. "Well!" I said. "That is quite a tale!"

"Yes." He was obviously pleased with himself. "It is, isn't it?"

"But what I would like to know is … "

"Yes?" he jumped on this. Was there ever, in the history of the world, a creature who so liked being asked questions? Who so liked knowing, more than anyone else, the answers to everything?

"But *how*?" I said, unable to stop myself from asking. "The last I checked, I knew everything you knew about the case, but now you know all this. You know all this … *information*, some of it going back decades! So how? *How* do you know all these *things?*"

"Because I read." More pleased. "Because I read and observe." More pleased still. "Plus, I'm incredibly nosy, and you take some incredibly long naps."

"What does *that* mean? The events you have been discussing mostly took place in America."

"That is true. You are no doubt deducing that as long as your naps may be, they are not long enough for me to make my way to America and back again. If so, you are deducing correctly."

I nodded firmly in response.

"Elementary, my dear Catson. During your naps, I made use of the telephone, calling America frequently to further my investigation. You may not care for the device, but I am rather fond of that invention of mine."

He –

Just how big was my telephone bill going to be?

Finally, most pleased of all: "Also, I visited Jefferson Hope in prison, not long after his arrest, one day while you were busily occupied with one of your longer naps."

Knock.

"Oh, and also?"

Knock. Knock.

"I know who that is at the door," he said smugly.

How could he? I looked around: the puppies, Mr. Javier, him, me. Wasn't everyone we knew already in this room? And yet:

Knock. Knock. Knock. Knock. Knock.

CHAPTER TWENTY-NINE

"I'll get it, Bosses! I'll get it!" Mr. Javier cried, rising from where he'd been taking a break from pretend dusting and, powered by his jetpack, flying with great speed down the stairs.

And …

… *crash*.

I know I said he had gotten much better with the device and it's true –he had – but there were still these occasional glitches.

After the expected "Ouch!," we heard the sound of the door opening, followed by Mr. Javier's enthusiastic greeting and the sound of muttering.

Then came the heavy, clodding tread of human footsteps on the stairs. Soon, Mr. Javier was back amongst us and – with him – the two public detectives: Inspector Strange and Inspector No One Very Important.

Eyeing our unusually large assembly, Inspector Strange said, "You know, I've gotten used to the idea of animals talking – well, just barely – but the turtle flying is still a bit much."

"Take your time," Bones said, "and with a little effort, perhaps you'll get used to that too. Now, what can we do for you fine gentlemen this evening?"

Fine? I didn't think they were so fine. And evening? Could it already be so late? A look outside the window confirmed that this was so. Where had the day gone? How could it have flown so quickly when so many hours had passed since my last nap? Usually, nap-challenged days take forever to live through.

"We have come," Inspector Strange announced to Bones, "to take you to prison."

"Well, you can't have him!" I cried, leaping up from my position in front of the fireplace and racing across the room more quickly than I would normally think my limp would carry me and hurling my body in front of Bones.

Never mind *fine* and *evening*, when had I grown protective of the dog?

"We're not hear to *arrest* him!" Inspector Strange said, laughing. Then he added the unfortunate words: "You silly feline."

I resented that.

"Then what do you want to take him to prison for?" I demanded, narrowing my eyes.

"Jefferson Hope has asked to see 'the great Sherlock Bones'," Inspector Strange said, clearly quoting Jefferson Hope but doing so with a high level of resentment and sarcasm. "Mr. Hope has not spoken since his arrest, save that one time he spoke with Bones shortly after, but now he says he is prepared to do so. He is prepared to tell all … but only to Bones."

"I knew this was coming," Bones said and, much as I hated to admit it, I believed he had. "Very well."

Bones rose to his feet and proceeded toward the

top of the stairs, only to turn back.

"Aren't you coming, my dear Catson?"

"Oh," Inspector Strange said, "no, no, no, no, no. That won't do. The prisoner said nothing of the cat."

"He will see her too or he will not see me at all. 'The cat,' as you so rudely put it, and I are partners. We are consulting detectives. Wherever I go, she goes. Well, except for when she is napping. Catson?"

With a soaring sense of pride – I never would have suspected I would ever feel *pride* at a compliment from the dog – I moved to accompany him.

And, as I moved, the six-pack of puppies and the flying turtle moved to move with me.

"No, really," Inspector Strange said, "no, no, no, no, no. I said yes to the cat because clearly Bones isn't coming without her, but I really cannot say yes to all of this."

The six-pack of puppies and the flying turtle cast their hopeful eyes upon Bones.

"I'm afraid I can't help you out with this one, lads and Mr. Javier," Bones said. "If we crowd the prisoner too much, it's likely he'll never talk."

"Oh!" Mr. Javier said with great disappointment. "I did so want to meet Mr. Jefferson Hope face to face, now that I know so much more about him. I feel so badly for him. Although I feel the need to point out that, no matter how good his reasons, you cannot just go around killing for revenge. No one should be allowed to do this."

"Yes, well," Bones said, "we shall tell you all about it later – I promise!"

And we were off.

CHAPTER THIRTY

We took a cab to the police station, following behind the inspectors, who had their own conveyance. As it happened, the horse drawing our cab was Fred.

"Do you see what I meant about Utah?" Fred said, as we loaded in.

"I did indeed, my dear Fred," Bones said. "That was very astute on your part. Don't you agree, Catson?"

"Oh, come on," I muttered, "it was just a lucky guess. Anyone can say *Utah* and just hope something will come of it."

The ride to the prison was not a long one. Once there, we entered through a side door, because Bones informed me that newspaper reporters regularly stalked the front door with their cameras and notebooks and pencils, hoping for a story. Inside, there were various members of the police hanging around, from detectives to uniformed patrolmen. As we passed by them, Bones striding proudly, I noticed they mostly regarded the dog with a grudging respect, although some regarded us with disbelief, even disdain.

"Now they're bringing a cat in too?" one derided to another. "What's next? A talking donkey?"

But the worst were the police dogs, the kind the humans use to catch the scent of criminals and such, sitting there in their matching navy blue jackets and caps with little tin badges. A couple regarded Bones with an amazement bordering on awe, but overwhelmingly they glared and scoffed at him. I heard some muttering about "acting too human" and "rising above his station." For some reason, this made me stand taller, stride more proudly at his side.

I did hear one of the humans call out, "I hear Moriarty's back in town," followed by a police dog yelling, equal parts insult and concern, "Yeah, what do you plan to do about that?"

This was the only thing Bones responded to, replying cheerily, "What I always do: handle the squirrel!"

At last, we were led to an interrogation room where the prisoner awaited us.

I had seen Jefferson Hope once before, when he'd been arrested in our home. And yet, somehow, I'd managed to forget he was so tall.

And very skinny.

Plus, he still had those incredibly tiny feet.

"My compliments to you, Mr. Bones," Jefferson Hope said in his American accent; during our first case, I'd noted that his accent had marked him as "not from around here," but I hadn't specifically noticed it being American. "You figured out what I had done so quickly. If I was in charge of your country, I'd put you in charge of all of the police."

Inspector Strange and Inspector No One Very

Important both turned red at this admonition.

"Thank you for speaking the truth," Bones said, with a nod, "although somehow, I doubt all would agree with your accurate assessment."

"About the truth," Jefferson Hope said. "I'm supposed to go to trial next week. Before that happens, I wanted to explain to you *my* truth."

"Why now?" Bones said. "Surely, it will all come out at the trial."

"Because I may not live that long," Jefferson Hope said simply. He made this shocking statement in a surprisingly cheerful fashion, as though not at all bothered by this fact. On the contrary, he seemed to welcome the prospect.

"What?" Bones said, for once surprised at something.

I studied the prisoner closely for signs. "It's true," I said at last, surprised at the wave of sadness that washed over me. But then, if the prisoner was not bothered, why should I be? "I am afraid that Mr. Hope is not long for this world."

How had I not seen it the first time I met him? It

was not all that long ago, a matter of a few weeks. I could still remember the annoying headlines in the newspaper afterword:

DOUBLE MURDERER CAUGHT BY POLICE!

But at the time of our first encounter, he had been so energetic, the sheer adrenaline of having been captured driving him to fight mightily for his own escape. Now I could see that what was once a skinny man had shrunken yet skinnier still. And that deathly pallor, his skin like dry ashes – it was not something I could miss now.

"I see," Bones said gravely.

"So you'll understand," the prisoner said, jocularly, "why I wish to make my full confession to you now!"

He coughed.

We waited.

"As Mr. Bones already knows, the two men you know as the Secretary and, er, John Smith – "

"Wait," I said stopping him. "*You* call them the Secretary and, er, John Smith too? But I thought that was just something *I* started." Which I had, as I wrote down in *Doggone*. "But we've never met before, not to have a conversation at any rate, so how could you … "

Jefferson Hope merely raised an eyebrow at me.

"Oh, right," I said, feeling slightly embarrassed. "Now I remember. Bones did say that shortly after your arrest, he visited you here one day while I was napping."

Jefferson Hope nodded meaningfully.

"That must've been when the dog explained to you how I'd come up with my own names for some people."

Another nod.

"Because, as I'm sure the dog no doubt told you, I have trouble with the names of some humans so I rename them with ones I can more easily remember."

Another nod, this one accompanied by an amused half-smile.

"So the dog briefed you on what those nicknames were so that, should we ever meet, it'd be easier for me to keep up."

And now there was nothing half about it as Jefferson Hope gave me a full smile.

If it were physically possible, I'd have blushed, I was so embarrassed. Then it occurred to me: there are far worse things in life than giving a dying man cause to smile wide, even if that dying man is a double murderer.

Then: "Is Lucy Fur even close to the real name of the woman you loved?"

"Oh, yes," he said. "Her name was Lucy and the man who raised her as his own daughter was named Joe. But the Fur part I did agree to because Mr. Bones said it would please you."

I didn't know how to feel about that.

"As I was saying," Jefferson Hope said, "and as Mr. Bones already knows, the two men you know as the Secretary and, er, John Smith were responsible for the deaths of two people I cared greatly about: Joe Fur and my beloved Lucy who, much to her sadness and mine, became Mrs., er, John Smith. Before she was buried, I took her wedding ring. It was in fact the ring I had given her when I asked her to be my wife. That scoundrel, er, John Smith couldn't be bothered to even get his own ring for her! You found that ring when you found the body of, er, John Smith, didn't you, Mr. Bones?"

Bones nodded.

"Having taken the ring," the prisoner continued, "I vowed upon it to avenge the deaths of the Furs. Toward that end, I chased them across two continents – North America and Europe – and I'd have chased them across all seven if need be, even Antarctica."

It was the second time that day I'd heard mention of Antarctica. How often does that happen?

"But that proved unnecessary," Jefferson Hope said. "Instead, I discovered they'd landed in England and so I came here myself. Arriving here, however, I discovered myself once again to be tragically low in funds. I needed more money if I was to continue my efforts, so I took a job as a cabdriver and I taught myself my own way around the city."

He coughed again.

We waited again.

"At last," he continued, "I found the Secretary and, er, John Smith. They were staying in a boardinghouse. But I knew I needed to bide my time. Attack the one in broad daylight and the other would be on to me. Even at night, if I didn't do it right, I might get caught before I could kill both properly. So again, I waited for my chance. Then, one day it came. I had trailed the two men to the train station and there, I overheard them fighting. I heard, er, John Smith shout, 'You're just a secretary!'"

Oh, I thought, *that must have smarted*. Even if the 'secretary' part was true, the 'just a' part had to have hurt.

"Well," he said, "after that, the two men separated. The Secretary went somewhere, but I wasn't paying much attention to him – not then. I knew I would be able to find him later. My first order of business was to attend to the man I held most responsible for the death of Lucy, the one who'd married her in my place."

We all paused for a moment of silence.

I could see that even after all these years, her loss

pained him greatly, as though it had just happened that very day.

"Now, as it happens," he went on, less sad now that he had returned to discussing his hunt for his quarry, "I had managed to secure a key to an abandoned house."

I knew that abandoned house! It was where we'd found the first body!

"Don't ask me how I got the key," he said with a dismissive wave of the hand. "At this point, I refuse to drag anyone else down with me."

I looked around the room and realized we all had to accept that this was the case. How, I ask you, can you compel a dying man – one who has already lost the dearest thing to him in this world – to tell you any more than he wishes to? Besides, there was no proof that the key provider was a criminal or had committed any wrongs.

"First," Jefferson Hope said, "I had to find a way to lure, er, John Smith to come with me. But in truth, that was easy enough. He needed a cab. I was a cabdriver! How much more simple could it be?"

"But didn't he recognize you?" I said. "Perhaps I only speak for myself here, but I can't imagine climbing into a horse-drawn cab driven by a driver who had pursued me across two continents and all over England."

I neglected to add that it was not my usual habit to climb into any horse-drawn cabs unless there was a compelling reason for me to do so, as there had been that day.

"You make a good point," the prisoner agreed, "except for a few things: one, I have this beard now, don't I?" He tugged on it.

It was an impressive beard but struck me as little more than the kind of flimsy disguise a human might don for a costume ball. Don't most people see through those things?

"And," he added, "two, twenty years of living hard can change a man's appearance considerably and that's what I'd been doing: living hard."

"I still don't see how – "

"And finally," he cut me off, "three, in the years I'd been chasing them, I'd been extraordinarily careful

147

not to let myself be fully seen."

Oh, I thought. *That might do it.*

"It's a funny thing," he mused, "but we humans, if we don't see someone for a long period of time – be that person friend or acquaintance or foe – when we do picture them in our minds, we see them frozen in time as they were the last time we saw them. Take, for example, if you have a friend when you are six years old and that friend moves far away. When you are ninety-six, should you get a chance to see that friend once more, you don't picture the meeting will involve an old man; you picture that it will involve the little boy you once knew."

"How perceptive of you, Mr. Hope!" Bones said with real enthusiasm. "That is why, in addition to inventing handcuffs on your behalf, I am similarly at work perfecting a device whereby if you have a picture of someone from some previous year, you can do this and that to it in order to make an educated guess as to what they might look like today!"

I wondered at that *this and that*.

"You are certainly the cleverest living creature

I've ever encountered, Mr. Bones," the prisoner said, "and I say only what I said before: The police would be lucky to have you in charge of them."

The police, once again, did not look pleased.

As for the prisoner, having said "I say only," as though he might say no more, he did in truth say more.

Quite a bit more.

CHAPTER THIRTY-ONE

Jefferson Hope asked for a glass of water. After one was produced, he continued:

"Once, er, John Smith was in my cab," he said after taking a sip, "I took him to the abandoned house."

"I would think," I said, "that he would be surprised to draw up in front of somewhere other than his requested destination, which I presume to have been the boardinghouse where he was staying. I further think his sense of surprise would not be a happy one."

I also thought: Why is the dog letting *me* ask all, or at least most, of the questions?

"You would think that," the prisoner said, "as most people would, and usually you'd be right. But, er, John Smith was always a greedy man – even his inheritance upon the deaths of the Furs was not enough for him. All I had to do was concoct a story about there being a bag of gold stored in the abandoned house, a bag of gold so big it was too heavy for just one man to carry. I offered to share half with him if he would help me get it all away."

I shook my head at this. "Greed," I said. "It always gets greedy people in the end, doesn't it?"

"It does indeed," he said. "Of course, once I'd led him far inside the abandoned house, I whipped out the wedding ring and waved it in his face so that *he'd* finally know who *I* was. And then I waved something else."

We waited.

And waited.

His cliffhangers were even worse than Bones's! And in his case and condition, was that really wise? If he let the cliff hang too long, he might be dead before he finished his story.

"Now," he said, "about that something else I waved. Here's something I perhaps should have mentioned earlier. I had obtained – again, I won't tell you from who – a certain amount of poison. Then I got some regular pills. I put the poison in two of the pills and left the other pills alone. Then I got two little boxes. In each box I put one of the poisoned pills and a bunch of regular pills. Are you with me so far?"

How could I not be? It was not exactly rocket science.

"I then compelled, er, John Smith to select one of the pills," he said.

I did wonder what form that compelling had taken.

"Just to be fair," he said, "I told him I would take one too. I can be as sportsmanlike as the next guy. Maybe he'd die. Maybe I would. Maybe no one would die."

In that moment, he seemed so cold-blooded.

"As it turned out," he said with a shrug, "he died. And very quickly I might add. Unfortunately, in my excitement and haste to get away, I accidentally dropped the ring, Lucy's ring."

"And you returned to the scene of the crime in an effort to get it back," I said, "but you couldn't because the police – not to mention Bones and myself – were already there."

"That's right. Although, as you know, I did get it back later. In the meantime, having gotten rid of, er, Mr. Smith, I went to the boardinghouse where I knew only the Secretary was now staying on the second floor. Although even I'm not tall enough to reach into a second-story window, there was a handy ladder nearby. Once inside, I gave the Secretary the same choice I'd given, er, John Smith, only using the second box of pills this time because the first box no longer contained any poison."

He made it all sound so matter of fact.

"Sadly," he said, "or perhaps not so sadly, the Secretary refused to go along with the you-choose-a-pill-first routine and he physically attacked me. I was therefore forced to do away with him in a different way which I can't say I minded that much, given he'd been the one responsible for the death of my beloved Lucy's adopted father. I stabbed him."

There was something about his next pause that made it clear he was coming close to the end, in more ways than one.

"Later," he said, "after both of the villains were dead, I thought I'd get away. But then a group of puppies came along. Their leader, a pup who introduced himself as Waggins, asked if I was Jefferson Hope and, when I said that I was, he told me a cab was required at 221B Baker Street. I thought it might look too odd, a cabdriver refusing a fare, so I came. And there you had me."

Yes. There we had him.

"But there's still one thing I don't understand," I said.

"And that is?" Mr. Hope said.

"You have given decades of your life, even sacrificing your health, and for what? Revenge?"

"You know, Dr. Catson," he said, his gaze moving to a corner of the room, a faraway look in his eyes as though he might catch one last glimpse of the past there, "before the day I met Lucy, I didn't believe in love, let alone at first sight. I didn't believe in it until it happened to me. But that day when I came upon her in trouble on her horse, and our eyes met? I knew I would never want to be without her again, and that she felt the same way about me. And then to lose her, before we could even be married? It was like I died then myself."

A part of me, having heard his tale, felt profound sympathy for the man. What would it be like to love someone like he had loved Lucy? What would it be like to hold on to that love for decades, over time and great distance, keeping only her in his mind as he sought to avenge her?

As I say, a part of me felt pity. And yet another, bigger part, remembered what Mr. Javier had said as we left the house earlier to come to the station:

"No matter how good his reasons, you cannot just go around killing for revenge. No one should be allowed to do this."

The turtle was right.

CHAPTER THIRTY-TWO

Having made his full and complete confession, Mr. Hope had no further need of us. As he had also signed a copy of that confession, the public human police had no further need of us either. So we were unceremoniously dumped out of the side door of the station without so much as a thank-you or a hail of a cab for us.

"Do you think Moriarty is responsible?" I asked.

"For what?"

"For Jefferson Hope being in a state of dying. Do you think the squirrel could have something to do with it?"

"I do not," he said. "You really must stop seeing the squirrel everywhere."

"Easier to do if he'd stop popping up everywhere!"

"He does not pop up everywhere! Besides, you're a doctor."

"True," I said. "I suppose, when we all met Jefferson Hope for the first time, we thought, 'Skinny man!' plus 'And now he's trying to escape out the window!' But chances are, he was already dying then. In some ways, I think he's been dying since he lost Lucy."

"It's a nice night," Bones said, turning up his snout to sniff the clean air. "We can walk."

Easy for him to say. He wasn't the one who normally had sixteen naps a day but today had yet to have any. He wasn't the one with a limp from the Cat Wars.

He must have seen me struggling to keep up, for he stopped and said, "Oh! Would you like a lift?" And then he did a shocking thing: he offered me a ride on his back.

A part of me was actually tempted. I don't care

for riding in horse-drawn carriages, as I've said, but then I don't usually know those horses. I did know Bones, however. Or at least, I was starting to.

But my pride would not let me accept. So I simply said, "If only you would slow that haphazard walk of yours, I think I can just manage to keep up."

I said this, of course, a little irritably. Heaven forbid the dog should get the idea I might actually be starting to not wholly mind him.

"As you wish," he said.

We carried on walking, but – to the dog's credit – a bit more slowly this time.

I did not thank him.

"Well, I think this is all just wonderful!" he burst out after a surprisingly companionable bout of silence.

"What is?" I asked.

"Isn't it obvious?"

"Would I ask if it were?"

"It's only this, my dear Catson: At last – at long last! – we *finally* know all of the why behind everything Jefferson Hope did!"

I thought on this. And, as I thought, I remembered something from the end of our first case together, which had really turned out to be this case too. It can be found near the end of my writing in *Case File #1: Doggone*, but for convenience sake I shall recount it here.

"But you said," I said, "after you first caught Jefferson Hope and I asked you why he did it, that the why didn't matter. That is what you said."

"Ah, it didn't then, but it does now, now that we do know. Have you never heard the phrase, 'that was then, this is now'?"

"I didn't then," I said wryly, "but I have now."

We walked on.

CHAPTER
THIRTY-THREE

The puppies and Mr. Javier may have been eager when we first left to hear everything that happened with Jefferson Hope. But that eagerness did not extend to waiting up several hours for our return. So, we found them all asleep in the living room when we arrived home: turtle and puppies all happily tangled together in one big reptile/canine heap.

Nor had they wakened by the time the dawn broke and, with it, the sound of the early edition of the newspaper hitting the door downstairs.

When we'd first arrived home, the dog needed to

roll around on his back for a while on the floor as he sometimes feels compelled to do, and I asked him to do so in his bedroom, so as not to wake the others. In reality, I'd wanted to make another telephone call outside of his hearing.

After he rejoined me, the dog and I had stayed up all night talking: about Jefferson Hope, about the previous cases Bones had worked on, about life itself. Now the dog looked at the sleeping turtle, no doubt hoping he'd wake to retrieve the paper, but the turtle was out cold.

"I suppose that I shall have to get my own paper this once," the dog said.

"And I suppose I shall have to make us tea," I said, padding off toward the kitchen.

"You can do that?" the dog said, incredulous.

"How do you think I managed during the Cat Wars?" I said. "You don't imagine I'd drag poor Mr. Javier into battle with me, do you?"

He still looked surprised and so I felt compelled to add:

"I, my dear Bones, am a feline of many talents."

CHAPTER THIRTY-FOUR

"Oh, look!" Bones said, snapping open the newspaper as I pushed in the tea trolley.

All around us still lay sleeping puppies plus the turtle, but I found that I didn't mind. Just this once, I didn't mind having a full house at all.

"What am I supposed to be looking at?" I said, pouring.

"The early edition is reporting that Mr. Jefferson Hope died in the wee hours, but that before doing so, he gave a full confession, cleaning up any loose ends concerning the double murder not too long ago."

I stood for a moment of silence at word of Jefferson Hope's passing. Then:

"What else does it say? Does it say that the confession was specifically made to you and I at the prisoner's request?"

"Don't be absurd!" the dog barked a laugh.

Absurd? Me?

"*They'll* never give *us* any credit! Not in *their* papers!" He stopped laughing long enough to say, "Of course, I don't imagine Inspector Strange or Inspector No One Very Important will be pleased either."

"No?"

"No. After all, the prisoner died before trial — where is there any splash in that?"

"Why should they get any credit or newspaper coverage anyway?" I demanded hotly. "Unless you include their wisdom in knowing they needed to consult you in the first place — *you* did it all!"

Oh my goodness. Did I say that out loud? Had I just defended the dog?

"I do thank you," he said, "for this surprising,

but of course wholly earned, display of loyalty."

Oh my goodness. Apparently I had!

"Giving credit where credit is due," he said, "that doesn't matter to the likes of them. But due to your great display of loyalty, I shall give you the gift of explaining a few things about detecting that should prove useful to you as we proceed along in our business."

I was already sorry I'd ever opened my big mouth.

CHAPTER THIRTY-FIVE

"Most people," the dog explained in an annoying instructional tone (it was pretty much how he sounded all the time), "think forwards. They think: Well, if this happens now, this is logically what will happen next. But to be a great detective, you must be able to think: If something has happened, what was the cause? Essentially, you must be able to reason backward until you arrive at the beginning."

"Can you provide an example?" I asked, half hating myself for my own curiosity.

"What could be easier?" he said, pleased. "Take

for example, Jefferson Hope. In his case, once I saw the first body and realized it had been murder, I moved in time directly backward from the body. From the body, I moved backward in time, outside of the abandoned building. There I found the tracks of a cab and two pairs of footprints: one tall, based on length of the stride; one not so tall. Since the dead body was not so tall, I concluded that I must look for the tall one as the murderer. I knew that having some idea of the motive would help me find the killer. It wasn't a robbery – there were still items of value on the dead body plus that gold ring in the room. But I did know from the ring we found that there was a woman involved. Since, er, John Smith did have identification on him, I asked Inspector No One Very Important to look into his background in the United States of America. Inspector No One Very Important being the sort of inspector he is, he, of course, neglected to do so. So I did it myself. That is when I learned of, er, John Smith's marriage to Lucy Fur, and her subsequent death soon after, and further learned that, er, John Smith had taken out a protection order against one Jefferson Hope. From there it was easy to conclude that Jefferson Hope was likely the tall man as well as the driver of the cab. Once a cabbie, always a cabbie – or at least for a little while, for it would have appeared too strange for him to suddenly stop. I sent Waggins and Company to ask for Jefferson Hope at every cab service in the city, and there you have it." He wiped one paw against the other. "Case closed."

CHAPTER THIRTY-SIX

"Except," I pointed out, "that while waiting to close your case, another man, the Secretary was killed."

"Details." He waved this off. "Jefferson Hope would have gotten to the Secretary regardless of how quickly anything else went. He was that determined."

Backwards reasoning, forward reasoning, circular reasoning: honestly, it seemed to me like he had used it all.

CHAPTER THIRTY-SEVEN

"**O**h, look!" he said as he continued scrolling through the newspaper. "Another item in the paper!"

"What does this one say?" I asked.

"It is an interview with the Superintendent, the head of all the police. In it, he praises Inspectors Strange and No One Very Important for their diligent police work. In fact, he calls that work wonderful. He also states that the double murderer Jefferson Hope, now deceased himself, was originally apprehended in the home of Sherlock Bones and Dr. Jane Catson."

My name should be first in that sentence, I thought. *After all, it's my name on the deed.*

"The Superintendent also said," Bones said, "that if the dog and cat played their cards right and listened to the likes of the inspectors, they themselves might one day be halfway decent detectives."

"*Halfway* decent? Halfway *decent*?" I was outraged on my own behalf; his too, come to think about it. "And that is why I never read the papers!"

Then I surprised him by laughing.

"What is so amusing?" he said.

I tapped the lower corner of the newspaper. "For such a good detective, I believe you were so distracted by the banner headlines that you missed this small article over here."

He followed my pointing paw to the small headline we could now read together:

BONES AND CATSON,
CONSULTING DETECTIVES, GET
FULL CONFESSION FROM HOPE

"That looks just as nice as I thought it would," I said, pleased.

The dog gaped at me, incredulous. "How did you – "

"Elementary, my dear Bones. I called in a favor from a cub reporter I know at the newspaper."

"A cub reporter?" For once, he was struck dumb.

"Yes, and by that," I said, "I really do mean cub. He's a young bear. I doubt they'll keep him long once he starts getting too big for the newsroom."

"But how did you – "

"Just because I don't bother reading the newspapers much, it would be illogical to assume I wouldn't know anyone who works for one. I simply phoned up the cub while you were rolling around in your bedroom – he works the late-night desk – and I told him what I wanted him to put in there." I admired the small headline again. "I think it's going to be good advertising for our business, don't you?"

"I – "

"Oh, and about those business cards."

"*Business* cards?"

"That's right. I phoned and ordered them yesterday while your little puppy friends were going bonkers over the takeout menus. The cards should be here in about two weeks, the stationers said."

ENDNOTE

Not long afterward, I did ask him:

"Will it always be like this? If there are more cases, will I think one is complete only to find out later there is still much to be learned? Like a second half?"

"I'm not sure what you're getting at."

"Will they all be two-parters?"

I was thinking about the Case Files I was writing down, but I could hardly tell him that.

"To be on the safe side," he said, "I would answer: You never know, my dear Catson. But realistically speaking: That is highly unlikely. I suspect, in our future, our cases shall be self-contained one-parters, in the main."

That relieved me somehow.

But then a new thought occurred to me.

"Way back in the beginning of yesterday, which was such an incredibly long day, you sighted that squirrelly squirrel, your nemesis, Professor Moriarty. And then of course you lost sight of him. Somehow, though, at the time, I thought he would figure into this tale. And yet, he has not, even though I did catch him spying through the bay window. Do you think he still will someday?"

"All I can say, my dear Catson, is watch and learn. Watch and learn."

How annoying.

Then I thought of my own thoughts about squirrels yesterday:

Devious. Highly intelligent. Incredibly organized. Deceptively adorable to humans. Not to mention, you never quite know what nefarious things one might be hiding beneath a bushy tail.

On top of all that, Moriarty was supposed to be

a criminal mastermind.

With a villain like that, one who had infected this last case with his presence throughout even though he hadn't necessarily done anything yet, how could he not appear in a mystery one day soon?

ACKNOWLEDGEMENTS

I wish to thank the following people for their help along the way:

Georgia McBride, for being a visionary publisher … and not just because we sometimes share the same vision!

Laura Whitaker, for being a visionary editor … and not just because we sometimes share the same vision!

Everyone at the visionary Georgia McBride Media Group – you're still rock stars.

My Friday night writing group plus my cat Yoyo, who's grown so comfortable with you all – finally! – that now he takes his own chair.

Greg Logsted: writer, husband and friend.

Jackie Logsted, daughter and the best reason to keep writing: so you stay proud.

Readers everywhere, but particularly readers who read Book 1 and have come back for more.

LAUREN BARATZ-LOGSTED

(Photo Credit: Jackie Logsted)

Lauren Baratz-Logsted is the author of over 25 books for adults, teens and kids, including The Sisters 8 series for young readers which she created with her husband and daughter. She lives in Danbury, CT, with that husband and daughter as well as their marvelous cat, Yoyo.

OTHER MONTH9BOOKS TITLES YOU MIGHT LIKE

SHERLOCK BONES 1: DOGGONE

Find more books like this at Month9Books.com

Connect with Month9Books online:
Facebook: www.Facebook.com/Month9Books
Twitter: https://twitter.com/TantrumBooks
You Tube: www.youtube.com/user/Month9Books
Blog: http://month9books.tumblr.com/

CASE FILE #1
THE ADVENTURES OF
SHERLOCK BONES
DOGGONE
LAUREN BARATZ-LOGSTED
AUTHOR OF THE SISTERS 8 SERIES